THE WEDDING RING
THE AUTHOR-PREFERRED EDITION

KRISTINE KATHRYN RUSCH

PUBLISHING

More Crime Stories

Every Little Thing

Morning Shift

Olivia's House

Stealth Bloggers

Take Your Daughter to Work Day

The Viral Video Guy

ALSO BY KRISTINE KATHRYN RUSCH

THE DIVING SERIES

Diving into the Wreck: A Diving Novel

City of Ruins: A Diving Novel

Becalmed: A Diving Universe Novella

The Application of Hope: A Diving Universe Novella

Boneyards: A Diving Novel

Skirmishes: A Diving Novel

The Runabout: A Diving Novel

The Falls: A Diving Universe Novel

Searching for the Fleet: A Diving Novel

The Spires of Denon: A Diving Universe Novella

The *Renegat:* A Diving Universe Novel

Escaping Amnthra: A Diving Universe Novella

The Court-Martial of the *Renegat* Renegades: A Diving Universe Novel

Thieves: A Diving Novel

Squishy's Teams: A Diving Universe Novel

The Chase: A Diving Novel

Ivory Trees: A Diving Universe Novel

Maelstrom: A Diving Universe Novella

THE RETRIEVAL ARTIST SERIES

The Disappeared

Extremes

Consequences

Buried Deep

Paloma

Recovery Man

The Recovery Man's Bargain

Duplicate Effort

The Possession of Paavo Deshin

Anniversary Day

Blowback

A Murder of Clones

Search & Recovery

The Peyti Crisis

Vigilantes

Starbase Human

Masterminds

The Impossibles

The Retrieval Artist

THE FEY SERIES

THE ORIGINAL BOOKS OF THE FEY

The Sacrifice: Book One of the Fey

The Changeling: Book Two of the Fey

The Rival: Book Three of the Fey

The Resistance: Book Four of the Fey

Victory: Book Five of the Fey

THE BLACK THRONE

The Black Queen: Book One of the Black Throne

The Black King: Book Two of the Black Throne

THE QAVNERIAN PROTECTORATE

The Reflection on Mount Vitaki: Prequel to the Qavnerian Protectorate

The Kirilli Matter: The First Book of the Qavnerian Protectorate

Barkson's Journey: The Second Book of the Qavnerian Protectorate

(coming 2024)

WRITING AS KRIS NELSCOTT

THE SMOKEY DALTON SERIES

A Dangerous Road

Smoke-Filled Rooms

Thin Walls

Stone Cribs

War at Home

Days of Rage

Street Justice

AND

Protectors

THE WEDDING RING

CONTENTS

Introduction   xiii

THE WEDDING RING   1
The Author-Preferred Version

THE WEDDING RING   73
The Originally Published Version

Afterword   137
Newsletter sign-up   141
About the Author   143

INTRODUCTION

Normally, when I put a collection together, I write full-fledged introduction, discussing my thinking as well as a little bit about the stories.

But for this edition, that essay shows up as the afterword. Otherwise, the introduction would be all spoilers. So if you want to know why I put two versions of this story into a single volume, you need to read the stories first, and then read the afterword.

I know. Rules, rules, rules.

The best crime fiction breaks them. Or at least, characters in the best crime fiction break the rules.

Serena will break the rules here. Just like Dylan did.

We start with the author-preferred version, followed by the story as originally published. And then the afterword.

Enjoy!

—Kristine Kathryn Rusch
Las Vegas, Nevada
December 12, 2023

THE WEDDING RING

THE AUTHOR-PREFERRED VERSION

ONE

The smell of coffee woke her. Serena stretched her arm across the soft sheets to find Dylan's side of the bed cold. She eased her eyes open. He'd actually pulled the covers up, and placed them under the pillow.

She smiled. In the five days they'd been married, he hadn't done that before. She had teased him a lot about leaving the bed unmade.

His answer was serious at first: *We're in a hotel, babe. They make the bed for us.*

Then he slowly realized she was joking. *They would make the bed, babe,* he said, *if we ever leave it.*

And finally, he said, *I'll make the bed the minute I know we're not going to use it.*

That last memory stabbed her heart. She sat up, covers pulled to her chest, something she hadn't done in six days. The room wasn't as dark as it had been; light filtered in around the thick curtains.

She blinked. The smell of coffee was strong. She made herself take a deep breath and smile. Dylan was in the other room, with room service waiting for her. He probably hadn't wanted to wake her. He'd done that the last two days, telling her that she needed her strength.

She *had* needed her strength, and honestly, her body needed a bit of a rest. She was getting all those honeymoon symptoms that doctors chuckled about. All it took, according to one of those websites she had accessed on her phone, was a little less physical contact for a day or so.

She had mentioned that to Dylan when he had asked what she was doing with her phone. He had smiled, said, *You're right, babe. We wouldn't want to hurt you permanently now, would we?*

And then he leered.

He had a good leer. She loved that leer, because of the twinkle in his eyes. He was the most handsome man she had ever seen—even after she had taken her beer goggles off.

She hadn't been drunk when she met him, but she hadn't been sober either. She'd been standing in one of the casino's beautifully decorated hallways, just outside the etched glass windows of the most popular nightclub in the place. She was wearing a slinky silver dress she had bought with her surprising slot winnings.

At the behest of the desk clerk when she checked in, she had taken one free pull on the gigantic slot machine in the lobby—and she'd won $10,000 instantly, making her eligible for a $100,000 grand prize three months out. Of course, she'd used some of her earnings to book the flight and the hotel for that new trip—just like the hotel planned—but the rest of it was found money.

She was cautious with her cash, always had been. She had put $5,000 in an account in a major bank here in Vegas, planning to transfer all of it and close the account when she got home. The remaining money (after she paid for her flight and hotel) was something she added to her vacation stash.

And the first thing she had purchased had been a dress so slinky, she felt like another woman.

She drank like one too, a little something every night, hoping it would give her courage—or at least, make this two-week trip a bit more fun. The trip hadn't started as a single-woman adventure. Initially, she had booked it for herself and her boyfriend of long-standing, Charles. When Charles ended their relationship three months before, she had kept the trip on the schedule because she felt like she had something to prove. In typical Charles fashion, he had told her during the break-up that they weren't intellectually suited, and he needed a woman of equal intelligence.

You're too smart for him, her friends had told her. *That's what he meant.*

But she had been there in the original conversation. He hadn't meant she was too smart for him. He had meant she was too stupid for him. And when it came to the biological sciences, she was. She didn't care about DNA, proteins, or the variations in some monkey's genome.

Once she'd even joked about that with Charles: *Dammit, Jim, I'm a professor, not a doctor.* But he didn't get it—a scientist who wasn't a *Star Trek* fan—and it was in that moment that *she* realized they weren't suited.

The *Star Trek* thing had occurred about a month before Charles ended it all. He had simply had more courage than she had. She had been worried about hurting his feelings; he hadn't been worried about hurting hers at all.

So she called this trip—one they had initially planned together (okay, she had planned it, thinking he would find all the math involved in casinos fun)—the Liberation Vacation.

Three days in, she'd been feeling a little more restless than liberated. She was feeling a little pathetic, and hoping no one noticed. The alcohol helped just a little, but only a little. It led to her dancing by herself in a casino corridor because she wasn't certain she could face the flashing lights and blaring noise and ultimate shocking aloneness of dancing alone inside the nightclub.

Then Dylan showed up—a blond god in a silk suit that fit perfectly.

He was romance-novel gorgeous, broad shoulders, muscular torso, narrow hips, a body which she later learned was as perfect unclothed as it was clothed. His hair was trimmed just enough to be stylish, not enough to make him look fussy. He wasn't wearing a tie when she met him, but he clearly had been just a little before. He had stuffed the tie in the pocket of his jacket, making him a little less perfect.

When he saw her, he had smiled at her, and extended his long-fingered hand. "A woman as pretty as you should never dance alone."

It had been a long time since someone called her pretty. In the beginning, Charles had said she was astonishingly attractive for an English major. But pretty? No one had called her that since high school.

Suddenly, the highlights she'd put in her hair, the weight she'd lost in the build-up to this Liberation Vacation, money she'd spent on the slinky dress she'd probably never wear at home were all worth it.

She was pretty, and a gorgeous man was smiling at her.

She took his hand, surprised and pleased to find calluses. He tucked her hand in the crook of his arm, and led her inside that nightclub. They'd danced and drank and laughed, and laughed, and laughed, and by the time they were done, their hands were all over each other.

She'd never been a public kisser, but she had been that night—hell, he could have taken her on the bar if he'd wanted to, because *she* wanted to. (He had said he didn't want them to get arrested at their magical first meeting.)

After the nightclub closed, they had gone to one of the casino's all-night restaurants, and had eggs and coffee. Then they decided that sitting in a booth was not what they wanted. They ended up in his hotel room first, and barely made it through the door before the suit and the slinky dress came off. Combustible sex, of the kind she'd only read about (the kind she thought authors made up), and then more sex, and some room service, and finally a bit of conversation, in which she learned that he was in Vegas to celebrate his own freedom—only his was a sad little freedom: his father had died two months earlier, and Dylan—his name was Dylan, after Dylan Thomas, the Welsh poet—had been his father's caretaker for the past two years.

Freedom, and liberation, and the surprising loneliness.

Oh, they realized they were kindred souls. He was footloose now that the estate was settled, and she had to go back to work, and, he said, he loved Denver, had always meant to live there—and he'd give it a try for her. By the end of the day, that "try" had turned into a certainty, and the two of them knew they couldn't live without each other.

The Elvis Chapel was a cliché she wanted to avoid, but they both wanted to marry immediately, thinking it romantic. No plans, no preachers, no haggling over the bests. No china patterns, no wedding invitations, just them—him in his silk suit (which they had to have pressed) and she in her slinky dress, commemorating the moment of meeting.

He bought her flowers—roses, despite the unusual deep cold in Vegas—and she bought him a matching boutonniere. They picked out expensive rings, with matching ruby stones and thick gold. He paid for hers, and she paid for his, and they clutched the boxes as they left the jewelry store, carefully located near some of the other chapels.

Only one looked like a sedate place. At the edge of the Strip, where the rents were probably still cheap, the building was small and tasteful with soft organ music playing in the front, and a lovely little white and gold backdrop used for photographs.

A substitute preacher married them—the regular guy was on his own honeymoon (*isn't that romantic?* the substitute asked with a comfortable smile)—and then they had a dozen photographs taken after they filled out all of the various paperwork.

Two days after she had met Dylan, she had married him. Her friends would hate it, but while he paid the preacher, she texted them photos—the chapel, pictures of Dylan from the side, the back, and then grinning at her as he walked up. The preacher gave them the actual photos and a disk with the images so they could print out more copies.

The paperwork would get filed in the morning (as soon as the courthouse opened), but, the preacher assured them, they were officially married as of midnight, January 15, as they signed their names to the lovely *Certificate of Marriage* to the organist's rendering of Bach's "Jesu, Joy of Man's Desiring," which, Serena thought, should have been renamed for the ceremony: "Dylan, Joy of Serena's Desiring."

This time, they had gone back to Serena's hotel because her winnings had earned her an upgrade to one of the suites, and a conversation with the front desk clerk had gotten them yet another upgrade—a honeymoon suite, complete with champagne, caviar, chocolate dipped strawberries, and two free room service meals.

She had ended up wearing the strawberries, and licking the caviar off Dylan's flat stomach, and laughing again, more than she ever had in her entire life. She hadn't given Charles a second thought until that fifth morning of her marriage, as the covers got pulled up to the pillow, the way Charles always left them when he deigned to sleep at her house.

She wrapped a robe around herself in case the smell of fresh coffee meant that the room service waiter was still in the room, and padded barefoot into the living room. The covered room service tray sat on the large table which she and Dylan had used for carnal purposes more than once.

There was no Dylan, and there was no note. She checked the bathroom, with the shower (with room enough for an athletic duo and maybe another), the bathtub (deep enough not to spill water even when someone was moving rhythmically), or the separate toilet area. She frowned, wondering where he had gotten to, when her image in the mirror stopped her short.

Her lips were swollen, her cheeks scratched by stubble, her gold-streaked hair messy. She looked well and thoroughly satisfied.

She smiled at herself—and then the smile faded as she realized what was missing.

Dylan's toiletries.

He'd spread them across the vanity—the special shampoo for his gorgeous hair, the shaving cream for his ultra-sensitive (and oh, so lovely) skin, even his toothbrush. All missing.

Her heart skipped a beat, and she thought she misremembered where they had been, but she hadn't. She knew she hadn't.

Maybe he had put them in the half bath near the door—she had teased him enough about his "products," since he actually had more than she did. Maybe he was hiding them because she embarrassed him.

Her friends had accused her more than once of having a sharp tongue. Maybe she had hurt Dylan more than she intended.

She pulled the robe tighter, and walked across the suite to the half bath near the door. This room was the only one that remained pristine, the only one she and Dylan hadn't used for anything except its intended purpose.

It looked lovely, with its little flower vase in one corner of the vanity, and the hotel toiletries on the other side. Who knew that the sight of a clean bathroom, beautifully decorated and absolutely perfect, would set her heart racing.

Racing and sinking at the same time.

She walked out of the little bathroom, her hands shaking now. Her body knew what her mind was refusing to acknowledge.

He wasn't here.

He had left.

But that wasn't possible. They loved each other. People who loved each other didn't treat each other like this. They didn't. They just didn't.

She walked quickly through the entire suite, suddenly angry that it was as large as the first apartment she had ever had. Lots of places to hide; lots of places to conceal things.

She looked in closets—empty except for her things. Her slinky little dress hung on a hanger, alone, not near his silk suit. He had said those two things should remain forever together in a closet or worn at the same time.

Their wedding clothes.

Her dress. Alone.

She swallowed hard, kept looking. His suitcase was gone. His toiletries were gone. His clothes were gone.

The bed was made.

There was no note.

Except...

She stomped to the dining table, and lifted the lid off the room service tray.

One meal. Eggs, lightly scrambled. Toast, dark. A slice of watermelon. An uncut banana for later. And a pastry for dessert.

Just like she liked it.

Like she had told him she had liked it.

And no note.

No damn note.

She flung the cover of the tray across the room. The silver cover clanged as it hit the wall, then clattered all the way to the floor. The sound was not satisfying.

Her lower lip trembled at the thought. The word. "Satisfied." The bastard. The fucking bastard. Literally.

Her eyes teared up, and she took a deep breath.

She was misunderstanding. She had to be.

She went back into the bedroom, and grabbed her phone, clicking it on, and froze.

It had reverted to factory settings. *He* had switched it to factory settings. All of her information was gone.

How had he gotten her password to unlock the phone?

And then she remembered him watching her as she opened her phone. Watching over and over again.

Her fingers shook, but she typed in all her information, then had the phone download her information from the cloud.

The phone told her that she did not have a cloud account. In fact, her phone told her she did not have any kind of account, and she had to sign up with a service provider.

She pulled the phone out of its case, saw the little scratch along the back that had been there since another case broke and her keys had defaced the phone's smooth surface.

It was her phone. But it didn't act like her phone.

She took a deep breath. It hitched. She took another, willing herself to remain steady.

Her purse sat on the chair near the window. She opened it.

Her wallet was there, and so was the cash. Her driver's license — *I'll have to change that when I get back*, she had said with a laugh the night they married, when she decided to take his name. His name. Jesus. His name.

She refused to let her mind go any farther down that road. She had her driver's license, her credit cards, her insurance card, everything. But she stared at it, afraid it would all bite her in ways she didn't understand.

She couldn't use her phone, but she could use the hotel's phone. In the closet, there was a phone book. Yellow pages, thank God. She couldn't remember the last time she had used paper yellow pages. She had always used her phone.

Bastard. Messing with her phone.

She flipped the pages until she found hotels and casinos, kept flipping until she found his hotel, the one she had watched him check out of. But maybe he hadn't. Maybe he—

She called the front desk of that hotel, asked for Dylan Thomas, and waited as the clerk checked.

"I'm sorry, ma'am," the clerk said. "We do not have a guest by that name."

She tried her last name, a variation on his name, asked the clerk to see if someone was using the same credit card that Dylan had used when he stayed there about a week ago.

The clerk's tone got frosty. "Ma'am, I'm sorry. We don't give out that information."

"He's missing!" Serena said, her voice suddenly sounding like someone else's. Screechy and terrified and watery, and oh, so devastated. Was she devastated? She didn't want to be devastated. She couldn't be.

She had only known him a week.

But she had married him.

The bastard.

"Oh, dear, ma'am," the clerk said and now her tone was sympathetic. "I'm afraid legally I can't just give this to someone over the phone, but we will work with the police on this. I hope you find him, ma'am. I'm sorry."

And then the clerk severed the connection.

Serena stared at the receiver as if the phone had caused Dylan to disappear. She made herself hang up. Hiccupping sobs threatened, but she wasn't going to allow them out.

She needed breakfast, but not the breakfast he had provided. She went back to the dining room table, grabbed the banana—the only thing that wouldn't have gotten cold or soggy—and then went to the bathroom with the gigantic shower.

She turned the water on scalding, stripped off the robe, and stepped inside, managing to control her mind until she lathered parts only a few other people had seen. Then she remembered the feel of Dylan's long fingers, the way he had learned (so fast!) exactly what made her gasp, what made her moan, and what made her slip into a frenzied lack of control that she had never experienced until him.

So talented, so amazing, so wonderful. So beautiful. Too beautiful for a mousy woman like her who had never been with a man so handsome. Too beautiful and perfect and—god, he had even smelled good. And his voice, so gentle, deep, and loving. She could almost feel him in the shower with her. She could almost touch him—

She whirled, hoping he was there, and of course, he wasn't.

And that was when she started to scrub—not just to get the feel of him off her skin, but the memory of him out of her mind.

Forever.

Two

S he didn't feel better when she got out of the shower, but she felt different. Raw, aching. Determined.

She toweled off her hair, looked at herself in the mirror, and saw—not the satisfied woman from earlier or the mousy English professor who had once dated Charles—but someone new, someone with flushed skin and flat eyes, someone who had an expression of sheer fury, and the look of someone who could do actual damage with that fury.

In the shower, she had come up with a plan.

She needed to call the police first. She had the sinking feeling that Dylan had taken everything from her, so she couldn't rack up charges on the hotel phone.

Once the police were involved, then she would work with the hotel. After she got started on that, she would find out what happened to her phone.

She would check her accounts, and if he cleaned them out, which she expected (God, she was stupid—and no, she wouldn't let that thought loose too much or she'd collapse in a sobbing puddle of uselessness)—*if he cleaned them out* (she thought loudly to herself, with emphasis, to control her emotional and unruly brain), she would pawn the damn wedding ring with its lovely stones that still glistened on her finger.

He had left her cash—five hundred dollars—which was something. Had he cared for her even a little bit? Or had he forgotten that she had cash?

She wiped her hand over her face. Emotions later. Situation first.

She sat on the hard living room couch, grabbed her mostly useless phone, and hit the emergency button. A keyboard showed up on screen, allowing her to call 911.

She did, and said, "I think I'm the victim of a terrible crime," and refused to burst into tears.

THREE

The police showed up fifteen minutes later. Two officers and a female detective showed up. The detective identified herself as Angela Castillo, part of the Las Vegas Sexual Assault Detail, which made Serena start. She hadn't reported a sexual assault.

She'd reported the marriage, the possible loss of everything, his disappearance, but not—

And then she flushed.

If her accusations were true (in the eyes of the police), and he had no intention of staying married to her, then—

She excused herself, went to the pristine small bathroom, and threw up.

Castillo stood in the doorway. She was in her forties, in shape, with caramel colored skin and dark eyes that seemed to miss nothing. She waited until Serena had cleaned herself up before saying,

"Come on. Let's talk alone. Where would you be the most comfortable?"

Castillo didn't suggest the bedroom, to Serena's relief.

Suddenly Serena wasn't comfortable there at all. But the bedroom wasn't the scene of the crime. The whole hotel room was the scene of the crime. The whole damn city was the scene of the crime.

Castillo looked at the officers. "Just give us a minute."

"No," Serena said. "We have to find him before he gets away."

"You don't know when he left?" Castillo asked.

Serena shook her head.

"Okay, a description, then, and his name. We can start there."

Serena gave his name, and his description to the officers. "I have a picture on my…" and then her voice trailed off. Her phone had been wiped clean. "Maybe with the papers?"

She had put the wedding certificate in her suitcase. She walked to the closet she'd been using, opened the suitcase, and the documents—which had been in a folder on top—were still there. She hadn't put them in the little pouch underneath where she usually put important information while traveling. She had been proud of that damn marriage certificate. She had looked at it whenever she opened the suitcase.

She pulled out the folder, opened it, saw the certificate remained, but there were no pictures any longer—at least not of him. One of her, the only one alone, *the bride shot,* the preacher had called it. She stood before the gold altar in her slinky dress, clutching the roses, matching roses beside her in large vases. She had looked pretty and happy and hopeful.

Naïve little idiot that she had been.

Serena swallowed. "He took them. All of them. Pictures and everything."

"Let me see," Castillo said, reaching for the folder.

She didn't look at the photo, but at the marriage certificate. Then she showed it to the officers who were also in the room.

"This isn't a valid marriage license." Castillo looked at the officers. "We're going to need someone from Financial and Property

Crimes ASAP. Tell the captain we need—oh, never mind. I'll call it in. You go down to the desk, ask to get copies of all of the security video for this floor for the last week, and this morning's video as well. See if we get a good image of this guy."

The officers nodded, and then walked out of the room.

"Let's sit in the living room," Castillo said. She had slipped on gloves. She was holding the folder now, with its one pathetic photograph, clearly waiting for Serena to make a decision.

Serena nodded, then followed Castillo to that hard couch. A sexual assault victim? But she'd give her consent. Over and over. And the sex had been good. It hadn't been coerced.

But it hadn't been what she thought either. It hadn't been the celebration of two people in love, two people who had found each other despite the odds.

It had been a joyous celebration by one, and a duty by the other. A duty he had been good at.

She frowned and rubbed her hands on her knees, feeling an ache throughout her body.

Dylan had violated her. Not sexually, not really. She would have wanted him, even for that one-night stand.

But he had violated her emotionally. Intellectually. Personally.

In every single way that counted.

Now, these revelations were taking her heart and crushing it. One little piece at a time.

FOUR

T he next few days were a blur of interviews, explanations, and bureaucratic horrors. Dylan had emptied her bank accounts, taken cash advances from her credit cards at the hotel casino—where she had identified him as her husband on that giddy first night (and every night thereafter, including just last night). He had taken an online second mortgage against her house.

Serena's house sitter had stopped a stranger from letting himself in—with Serena's keys—so that he could help himself to her belongings. The stranger had looked nothing like Dylan. (*Believe me*, Serena's sitter said. *I would have remembered a handsome blond. This guy was short and dumpy and smelled of onions.*)

Dylan had taken the sim card from Serena's phone, replacing the card with another. He hadn't wiped the memory as much as stolen everything about the phone that made it Serena's.

Except he hadn't known about the automatic cloud backup. Once the helpful man at the cellular store had helped Serena reset her phone, the cloud downloaded, with a few extra treasures.

Photographs of Dylan, not the ones in the memory—he had clearly deleted those at night while she slept—but buried in the texts she had sent her friends. She had forgotten about those, and told Castillo about them.

The other detective Castillo had brought in, a hard-faced woman named Kree, had asked for permission to dig through the phone. The phone was where Dylan had gained most of his access. He had everything of Serena's, from her social security number to her passwords, neatly stored in a little unmarked book which she had shown him, a book she kept in a pocket on her suitcase (with another copy at home).

He had emptied her accounts the day he left, but the other things—the second mortgage, the new credit cards in her name, the credit lines he had opened with her very stellar credit number —those had all happened while she slept, sated, from their lovemaking.

She said, as Kree revealed more and more, *he screwed me even while I was asleep.*

Castillo had looked at Serena with empathy. Kree had looked at her with hard-edged pity. Serena had the sense before the end of the first day that Kree believed most financial crime victims got exactly what they deserved.

But Kree was efficient and helpful. She got the new credit lines and second mortgage cancelled, got the various banks to absorb all of the losses except the important ones—at least to Serena. The actual cash he had taken from her accounts he had done with her written permission, using the signature she had stored in her phone, and he had done so while she thought she was still married to him (albeit, in the hours before she realized what he had done).

At Kree's advice, Serena consulted with an attorney (one free hour, thankfully) and the attorney said that withdrawing permission after a major fraud had occurred was often hard. Especially since Serena had been in Dylan's company when the fraud happened. The banks would probably sue on that one, the attorney had said, and while they wouldn't win, they would tie her up in court.

Besides, he added, probably thinking he was being helpful, even if the courts ordered the banks to repay her, the amount of money she had lost—in the five figures, not six—would probably have been eaten up in additional expenses, and that was supposing the bank paid her court costs. If the bank didn't pay her court costs, she'd lose even more money.

Much as this attorney wanted to represent her, he said, she would be better off writing off the losses and beginning again.

His words were harsh; his manner hadn't been. In fact, he had apologized several times, as if he were personally responsible for Dylan's actions.

Everyone was kind to her, and with the exception of Kree, treated her like Dylan had broken her. Serena was beginning to like Kree more and more.

Kree didn't care about Serena's emotional state. Kree wanted to put Dylan away.

"This is incredibly organized," Kree said one afternoon when Castillo wasn't in the room. "This Dylan guy had a team. The substitute preacher, the guy at your house, I'm sure there were others. And they targeted you and played you. They've done this before. Just not in Vegas."

"I-I'm the first?"

"Here, it seems," Kree said. "We can't find any evidence of this happening to someone else. I have an associate reaching out to the hotels to see if someone reported something like this to them, but the hotels should call us if they realize that a major fraud ring is working the city."

"Maybe the women involved didn't report it," Serena said,

trying not to wrap her arms around her torso. She'd been doing that a lot lately, the lonely woman version of a deep and comforting hug. "It's pretty embarrassing. I mean, who would think—"

"Do you know how many people elope in Vegas with someone they just met?" Kree gave her that flat stare. "Enough so that at any given time, there are at least fifty wedding chapels in this city. Fifty. And not everyone plans ahead for a Vegas wedding. A good half of the weddings here are between drunks who just met."

"Thanks," Serena muttered, knowing Kree believed Serena fit that description. She didn't want to correct Kree's misperception. Serena hadn't been drunk at her wedding—at least with alcohol. When she had awakened after that first rapturous night with Dylan, her beer goggles gone, he was even prettier than he had been when she was tipsy.

She had fallen in love, and fallen hard, and she had married this man—this handsome predatory creature—she had married him stone-cold sober.

"That's what's bothering me," Kree said, ignoring Serena's slide into self-pity (which Serena liked; it was enabling her to ignore her slide too). "With this many wedding chapels, and so many lonely whatever-happens-in-Vegas-stays-in-Vegas women coming every single day, we should have encountered this crew before. And we haven't."

"If they're not local, how did they get the chapel?" Serena asked.

"He really was a substitute preacher, hired for two weeks while the regular guy went on vacation," Kree said. "Of course, all of his information was false. It went deep enough that a cursory background check which the chapel owner would have done would have seemed on the up-and-up."

"So everyone there—?

"The regular organist was sick that night," Kree said. "Severe food poisoning, which she got two days into the substitute preacher's gig."

"You think he did it," Serena said.

Kree nodded. "Like I said. Organized. We're bringing in the FBI on this. They have a crackerjack financial fraud team, and since this ring crossed state lines by going after your Denver house, they'll be handling a lot of the case."

"You're not?" Serena felt like she was losing her lifeline, and she had only known Kree a short time.

For the first time, Kree smiled at her. "I'm sticking on this one, whether the feebies like it or not. What these guys did to you..."

Kree shook her head, then bit her lower lip. Her entire body was rigid with fury.

Serena admired that fury. She wanted some of it. Right now, she was numb, just getting through. But that fury looked mighty attractive.

"What those guys did to you," Kree said after a moment in which she took control of her voice, "that was personal. Getting to know you, *seducing* you. They didn't just steal the identity of a name on a credit card. They took your identity, made you volunteer to get a new name, and let you think you were walking into the sunset with the man of your dreams. They're not in this for the money. They're in it to destroy their marks. *That's* unacceptable. We have to catch them before they do it again."

Serena's throat had gone dry. She had to swallow three times before she could speak.

"They didn't destroy me," she said, but her voice sounded almost like a whisper. Broken. Ruined.

Kree looked at her.

Serena swallowed again. "They *didn't*. I'm right here. And I'm going to destroy them right back."

FIVE

Kree and Castillo went straight from sympathy to what they called an intervention. They signed Serena up for some local counseling, since they still needed her in Vegas for a few days.

"Revenge is not the solution," Castillo said. "You need to heal."

Kree, at least, understood the need for the revenge, but worried about Serena doing it herself. "I'll keep you in the loop," Kree said, "but you let me do the dirty work."

Serena nodded as they spoke. She would go to the counselor. God knew, she did need help to deal with all of this.

But the first time she felt alive since Dylan left (since the bastard abandoned her) was when she said she would destroy him. She had said *them*, but she meant *him*. She would find him, and she would ruin him.

She just didn't know how.

And as she started to give it some thought, she realized she had no idea how to ruin a man with no real name, no real reputation, and no real sense of shame.

She would have to ponder that.

In the meantime, she had a lot of clean-up to do. The first thing she did upon return from the police station was move to a different room. The hotel comped it, as if they were responsible for Dylan. Castillo called their behavior "nice." Kree said that the hotel simply wanted to keep Serena as happy as possible so she wouldn't sue.

Serena had no idea what she'd sue for—the hotel hadn't introduced her to Dylan—but, Kree said, Serena had met him there, and that alone might have been enough for someone to sue.

If Serena were the suing type, she would have sued the hotel, the chapel, the nightclub, *everyone*, but she wasn't that type of person. Besides, suing everyone just blamed the wrong people. The person most at fault was her. Kree had been right about that (even if she hadn't said it directly). Serena should have known better, should have realized that the man she married, *on the rebound, for godsake*, wasn't who he appeared to be.

But he bore a lot of the responsibility too. What kind of human being was he? How could he soothe her hair from her forehead, listen to her secrets, learn how her body responded, all the time knowing the hurt he would cause her? What kind of person did that?

The new room was in a different wing, with different décor. She still had a suite, but it looked nothing like the old suite, and she was grateful for that. She had moved her own suitcase, after the police were done with it, and as she hung up her clothes, making the room a hundred percent hers, her fingers ran across the almost-invisible zipper beneath her clothes.

The pouch where she stored her important papers while she was in a hotel room. She always removed them and put them in her purse when she got on a plane, but she had—before this—always calculated her odds of being robbed. She figured if she left the papers in the suitcase and the suitcase went through airline security (unsupervised), she could be robbed by a determined airline employee. If she left them in her purse in Vegas while walking down the street, she could be robbed by a mugger. If she put them in the hotel safe while she was out, she could be robbed by hotel staff.

She hadn't expected to be robbed by her own husband.

Serena took a deep calming breath, something that still wasn't habit yet, and made herself open the pouch.

The documents for her new money market account—the one she had set up for taxes and incidentals from her win the day she arrived—were still inside. Her fingers lingered over them. She hadn't told Dylan about this account. She had told him that she had saved some of the money for taxes, and they could spend the rest, but she hadn't told him she had started a new account to hold that money separate from everything else.

She would have told him, but it had slipped her mind. *He* had made it slip her mind. She smiled, feeling the first ray of hope in days.

She grabbed her phone to check the account, then realized she hadn't set up online banking for that account. She hadn't planned to have the account long enough to need all the online services, so she hadn't set them up.

Instead, she called the bank using its 800-number, that old system that felt so twentieth century now.

After she punched in more numbers than she cared to think about, she came out with a piece of information that made her giddy: She still had the full $5,000 of her winnings.

She suddenly didn't feel broke anymore.

She certainly had less money than she had when she started all this, but she wasn't going to live paycheck-to-paycheck, like she had feared.

She let out a shuddery sigh and sank down on a nearby chair. Dylan hadn't taken *everything*, the damn bastard. Only because he hadn't found it all.

That realization gave her an odd feeling of power. He hadn't entirely outsmarted her. He wasn't totally brilliant. He could be defeated.

She could defeat him.

She just had to figure out how.

Six

Her first order of business was to put her life back together. Which sounded easier than it actually was. After the police finished with her, after she found a legal counselor and a financial advisor and a fraud specialist who was going to help her repair the damage that Dylan had done, she had to leave Las Vegas.

She was happy to do so. More than happy.

But her home, a Victorian on a twisted street in historic Denver, didn't feel like home any longer. It felt like it belonged to another woman—and essentially, it had.

That woman had been content dating Charles forever. That woman hadn't broken up with him quickly to spare his feelings. That woman had thought a trip could empower her.

That woman had had a quiet life—a good life—and hadn't even realized it.

That woman was dead.

Serena sold the house quickly and for a good price. Instead of putting all of the money in the bank, in an account someone could break into, she scattered it through a variety of investments, none she tracked on her phone. She bought a luxury condo in downtown Denver, on the upper floors of one of the luxury hotels, figuring if she decided to leave the city, she could rent the damn place out.

The condo looked nothing like her old house. The condo was modern, with white walls and spectacular city views, stainless steel appliances, and interior bedrooms that had a whiff of hotel design to them. She didn't care. She dumped her old furniture, bought new for the condo, and added some modern art, something the old her would have hated. But she liked the jagged edges and the bright bold colors.

She upgraded her wardrobe too, trendy items, as trendy as her condo, and as brightly colored as the paintings. She took night classes in computers, learning the ins and outs of the internet, occasionally cringing at all of the mistakes she had made with her privacy B.D. She had decided to refer to her entire past as B.D.

Before Dylan. Before Disaster. Before Deciding to change.

She was going to quit her job soon, but no one knew that except her. She had to struggle to pay attention to the classics. Really, who cared what Charles Dickens was thinking when he wrote *A Christmas Carol?* It was interesting to learn the first time, that he'd written the damn thing for money back when he was nearly broke, but repeating that story semester after semester to dull-eyed English majors who pretended to read the novella but really just watched a bunch of films wore her down.

She wasn't a professor anymore. She didn't care if the little shits learned anything.

Not that knowing the life of Dickens would help them in the real world. After all, Dylan might have named himself after Dylan Thomas the Welsh poet, but that little detail had been a weapon he used against her, just like all the other details he had used.

Her friends were trying to slow her down. They complained when she sold the house. They complained when she moved. They complained when she cut her hair. They complained when she got new clothes.

When they complained too much, she stopped calling them. She wanted to say she made new friends, but she really didn't. She made new acquaintances, people she could laugh with in the bars near her condo, people whom she watched get drunk while she stayed startlingly sober. She learned to sip her wine—no more guzzling beer, no more mixed drinks, no more nothing—and she learned to watch.

She saw pickpockets and working girls (although they preferred to be called escorts). She saw the scammers and the flim-flam artists. And she realized just how rare Dylan had been.

Usually women ran his kind of scam—not the marrying part, but the sex part. Using desire to get not just in someone's pants but into their wallets as well. Most of the women did it in one night, and many of them got arrested.

No one, so far as she could tell, ever managed to marry and scam—except those men who had different wives in different states, something she slowly learned was a different pathology altogether.

She made a study of con artists and bar behavior. When she wasn't watching people, she explored the internet, searching for a familiar face, searching for a pattern.

One after another, her counselors fired her. *You don't seem to want to get better*, one said to her.

I didn't know I was ill, Serena said in return.

You have no desire to explore your own healing, another counselor said.

I've repaired my life, Serena answered.

No, the counselor said. *You* changed *your life. That's not the same thing.*

Serena hadn't argued the point, although she could have. *She* hadn't changed her life. Dylan had. From the moment she met him. The fantastic sex (which she still sometimes dreamed about), the fake marriage, the hopes for the future—all came about because she met Dylan. That this particular happily-ever-after ended with the princess getting screwed royally by someone posing as Prince Charming didn't alter the fact that the chance meeting in the corridor outside the nightclub would have changed her life no matter what.

She kept hiring counselors, though, mostly as someone to talk to. On her eighth counselor, she finally figured out how to use the system. She talked sideways about Dylan, about what kind of personality he had to have, about what made him tick.

If she figured out what kind of person he was, she lied to the counselor, she would heal.

This particular counselor bought the argument for exactly two sessions. The next counselor for three. The next for another two. They argued that her healing had nothing to do with Dylan, and she privately begged to differ.

As they spent the hours she paid for analyzing him, she learned a few things.

She didn't believe the counselors who sympathetically said he had probably been sexually abused as a child or that he had a pathological hatred of women. She'd met a few men who hated women. It always came out sideways.

The counselors she believed were the ones who called him a sociopath. He had the charm and the charisma, the lack of interest in society's rules, and the love of putting one over on others.

He clearly had done that with her.

The problem was that people like Dylan felt no remorse, guilt, or shame. They blamed others when caught. So all of the FBI's work in finding him, all of the work Kree was doing and keeping Serena apprised of, wouldn't devastate Dylan, even if he was arrested. He'd be disappointed, but he'd blame all of them for his situation, not himself.

Sociopaths, one counselor said to Serena, *are all about control.*

And that, that little sentence, that one small idea, reverberated through her head for weeks.

Control. She had ceded control to him, and he had taken control of everything else.

But he had made it a game. From the name, Dylan Thomas, to the sex, to the pretend marriage.

It had all been a game.

And games were all about winners and losers.

After she had that realization, her smiles became real, and her determination became strong.

She dropped the counselors and made finding Dylan her number one priority.

SEVEN

It took nearly two years and a lot of focus to find him. Even then, she wasn't certain she had found the right crew.

She used the information she got from the authorities, but she never gave them any information in return. The FBI had found a pattern—the crew would hit an area, usually with a casino, but not always; often with a great nightlife, but not always; sometimes with relatively simple marriage license requirements, but not always.

The reports were fewer than reports on most fraud crews, because of the thing that Serena had said: women were often embarrassed to admit they were taken. Some even hired a divorce attorney only to learn that they hadn't really been married in the first place.

The FBI searched for a pattern, Kree watched for their return to Vegas (while keeping Serena apprised) and Serena employed increasingly more sophisticated facial recognition software as she searched likely areas.

She hooked up with a hacker group online, learned how to get into hotel security cameras, and make traffic cameras near hot spots do her bidding.

The FBI made a map of where the crew had been, and Kree had forwarded it. Serena looked at the pattern and did exactly what the authorities did: she tried to figure out where the crew would go next.

But they had to wait for a crime.

She didn't.

And she had the benefit of knowing not just what Dylan looked like, but how he moved, how he slid through a crowd, how he touched women. She also knew what the substitute preacher looked like.

But that didn't find Dylan for her.

Three patterns did.

In the towns without overnight wedding chapels like Vegas, the substitute preacher set up a website for his marriage services, and attached it, like a barnacle, to the regular county clerk's office site. When engaged couples figured out that they wanted to marry, the website would send them to the preacher to set up his bona fides. It took a little time, but this crew seemed to have nothing but time.

That, combined with the travel pattern the FBI figured out, helped her find the preacher.

But it was Dylan's ego that helped her find him.

He assumed he was smarter than everyone else, prettier, smoother, better educated. In one town, he was Bob Browning. In another, Edward Cummings. And with Serena, he had been Dylan Thomas.

Famous male poets—Robert Browning, e.e. Cummings. Dylan Thomas.

If the mark knew the name, like she had, Dylan copped to it—

my parents named me for the poet. If the mark didn't, no one said a word.

And no one else had noticed, except her.

She kept a list of poet names, and had various online alerts set up so that she could track the arrival/appearance of one of those names in the systems of the hotels in the locales that should've been next on the list.

The crew had a system that the FBI found. The crew would go to one city per state, never more than one in a trip, and never to adjoining states. So after they had left Serena in Las Vegas, they went to Washington State, skipped over Idaho and Montana, and ended up in the Dakotas. They never visited the same state in the same year, but they seemed to have favorite states, Nevada being one of them.

Two years, which meant they were due. And after they left Florida, Serena knew they would start all over again. Only they didn't backtrack. They always went west to east, never east to west. They would skip California, because they always seemed to skip California, which was leading the FBI to believe that the crew had history there, history that probably meant they didn't want to do anything to alert the California authorities.

The FBI was investigating that angle, or so Kree said, but they had little to go on. Serena didn't care about that angle. She cared about catching them in the act.

She had a plan.

And when a blond, exceedingly handsome John Donne checked into the priciest hotel on the Las Vegas strip, she knew she had him.

EIGHT

Serena did not tell Kree or Castillo that she was returning to Las Vegas. She simply arrived. On the flight from Denver, she watched the hotel's security footage over and over again. She hadn't needed her special illegal facial recognition software to recognize Dylan. She knew every inch of that face, and even after she had cleaned up the security footage, she knew that his appearance hadn't changed at all.

Hers had. She was thin to the point of bony, her hair darker and longer. She no longer fit into the slinky dress (yes, she'd kept it) because it was too loose, and her wedding ring (yes, she'd kept that too) spun on her left finger.

She'd wrapped yarn around the back of the ring as if she were a teenager, but after she'd checked into a different megahotel across South Las Vegas Boulevard from Dylan's, she scouted hair boutiques so that she could get hers wedge-cut and lightened. She didn't do it immediately—she didn't want Dylan to recognize her (even though she doubted he would)—but she did buy another slinky dress. It wasn't quite the same as the original, although she and the saleswoman looked and looked for the same model, but it was close. Same color, similar style, hard for anything except the experienced eye to see it.

Serena had the same shoes, however. She could reappear as her old self at any point. "Old self" wasn't quite accurate: she had only been that slinky blond self for six days, six marvelous delusional days when she thought the fairy tale would never end.

She had no idea how Dylan picked his marks, although she had a theory. She had won that jackpot at the beginning of her stay, two years ago, and babbled to the hotel staff like an idiot about the Liberation Vacation and how it was starting perfectly.

Over the years she (and the FBI and Kree) all doubted that Dylan had a crew member on staff, so that meant that he watched for some lucky hapless woman to reveal her loneliness in a painful and public fashion.

He had to spend his days watching for her.

Serena set up a wireless station inside her hotel room, so she didn't have to use the hotel's creaky old system. And she watched the lobby for a few hours before realizing that Dylan wasn't down there, but someone else was.

A short, dumpy guy who looked like he might actually smell of onions moved around the lobby, monkeying with his phone, sitting in a chair, going in and out of the nearby hotel gift shop. Serena didn't know for certain because she had no pictures of the guy, but she was pretty sure that the man she was watching was the same one who had let himself into her house two years before using her own keys.

He finally left the lobby about four hours in, and it didn't look like anyone had replaced him. Which meant he'd found the right mark.

She reviewed the footage, wishing she had audio as well as

video. People—especially nervous people—revealed too much when they were checking into hotels.

She ended up with three possibles—all not-quite-pudgy blondes who looked both lonely and nervous—and watched the dumpy guy's reaction to them. He kept his eye on one for a tad too long. Serena was going to go with her, until she realized that he wasn't looking at the pudgy lonely woman. He was looking at a willowy blonde who seemed ever-so-slightly angry.

The willowy blonde smiled and laughed as she checked in, but the desk clerk looked a bit uncomfortable, the way people did when they heard too much information about someone they didn't know. Then the blonde held out a sparkling diamond ring, shook it at the clerk, and laughed again.

The clerk shrugged, took out a map, and circled someplace on it.

Serena's breath caught. She would bet her last dollar that the blonde wanted to sell that ring. Not pawn it. Sell it.

They weren't targeting lonely women. They were targeting *angry* women traveling alone. After all, what had Serena and her Liberation Vacation been if not angry? She had just been too repressed to admit it using words like "anger" and "furious." Instead, she had made jokes about her trip.

That woman really was gone. If Serena was angry these days, she said it, in no uncertain terms.

She had moved beyond anger with Dylan. Somewhere along the way, her fury had turned from a red-hot rage to something more akin to a dish served cold.

She hacked into the hotel's system, saw that the blonde—one Nicole Warrington—had checked into a suite that had been booked months before, and knew, knew, she was looking at Dylan's next "wife."

If Serena were still a good little girl, she would have called Kree and Castillo and alerted them. But she wasn't. Kree and Castillo would screw everything up.

If they asked later, Serena would say that she wasn't certain what happened to Dylan after she saw him check in.

And if she were honest with herself, she wondered why he was in the same hotel as the mark.

Or maybe he wasn't. Maybe he had gotten the room as insurance, let the dumpy guy use it, and had also gotten another room at a different hotel. That other room would also be under the name John Donne—if, indeed, he was running the same scam.

She would search for that in the morning. Just like she would try—again—to search wedding chapel "pastors." That was harder. Even though the chapels had online advertising, their websites were mostly static, and their business was in-person, so she couldn't figure out if they had hired someone new or gotten a substitute preacher, like they had when she had arrived.

She knew that Kree monitored the original wedding chapel, but Serena doubted the crew would use the same chapel twice.

She stayed in her room, ordered room service, and watched security footage until she saw Nicole Warrington leave her suite in a gorgeous red designer gown that showed every single curve to great advantage.

Nicole Warrington looked like a woman trying to shake off a man any way she possibly could.

She looked stronger than Serena had been. Angrier. (Prettier.)

For several heart-stopping minutes, Serena worried that Nicole would go to a nightclub outside of the massive hotel/casino complex.

But her worries faded as Nicole marched down to the most expensive nightclub inside the complex. Dylan would have to work quickly to catch this woman, because other men would be lined up.

Serena hoped he would work the corridor again, because seeing what he was doing inside the nightclub would be hard. The place had security, but it also had dim lighting that was punctuated by strobe lights when the music demanded it, and she would have trouble seeing faces.

Nicole Warrington went inside, and Serena didn't see Dylan at all.

She let out a breath, wondering if she had focused on the wrong mark.

She didn't want to miss this opportunity, and she was just afraid that she might.

NINE

There was only one real exit to the club, which Serena monitored for four hours. While she watched, she worked on a second screen, searching lower-tier hotels for John Donne. She almost missed him. Facial recognition didn't find him, because he wore a ball cap low over his face, and he didn't register as John Donne.

He registered as Jonathon Donne.

The thing that confirmed it for her, though, was as she watched the security footage, she saw him roll the keycard over his fingers, just like a poker player rolled a card. He had done that with her keycard (their keycard?) more than once.

Her heart pounded as she watched, and she knew now that she was on the clock.

She had started reviewing the front desk footage for the mega-hotel when Nicole Warrington staggered out of the nightclub. Serena let out a breath. She had forgotten: the mark had to be drunk or at least tipsy before Dylan would approach.

And then he came out, perfect in a gray suit that shimmered in the soft light. Nicole saw him, laughed, and extended her hand. Then they exchanged a kiss that Serena could almost taste. She remembered kissing Dylan like that, and wrapping her body around his just like Nicole was.

At the moment, it looked like Nicole was in charge, not Dylan. He looked like the perfect goofy pick-up, the guy who couldn't believe his luck. They kissed again, and she slid her hands under his suitcoat and down. His entire body jerked just slightly as her fingers must have found what they were searching for.

He shoved her against a wall, cupped her butt with his hands, and brought her forward.

A hotel security guard tapped him on the shoulder, and clearly told them to get a room.

They laughed, and staggered away. They headed to her room, which surprised Serena. Dylan had convinced Serena to go to his, although she couldn't remember how. Maybe she had balked at bringing him to hers. She probably had, with her old paranoia about being robbed.

Not that anyone was thinking of robbery at that moment, except maybe Dylan. He had his back against the row of mirrors inside the elevator, and was letting Nicole unzip his pants. She tugged up the front of that slinky dress. They weren't going to make it to the room.

Serena watched with horror. The entire act happened fast, and she knew it had ended, at least for Dylan, when his head turned upward and his face grimaced in a way so familiar to her that she felt it in her heart.

That was *her* look. He had reserved it for *her*. No one else was supposed to see it.

She had to get up and walk away from the computer, her entire body shaking.

She had just become jealous. This wouldn't work if she were jealous. Dammit, she still had feelings for that man, buried deep, but not as deep as she thought.

And instead of wanting to save and help Nicole, Serena felt herself wanting to eviscerate the woman, take that slutty red dress and—

Serena made herself breathe. Dylan was not her husband. He wasn't even named Dylan. He was some man, some horrible man, who had just targeted another vulnerable drunken woman, and just because his play-acting remained the same didn't mean that he loved her any more than he had loved Serena.

He didn't love anyone but himself.

Serena sat back down and reversed the video just a bit, to that expression on Dylan's face. She froze the frame and made herself stare at it.

This is the face of a man who exchanges sex for money, she reminded herself, mouthing the words as she thought them. *This is the expression of a man who gets off on using people for his own purposes. The excitement of screwing a mark meant more to him than the sex act itself.*

She didn't quite believe it, not the way her heart hurt, so she made herself rewind and view it again. And one more time. But the ache didn't lessen, and while her head knew what that son of a bitch was doing, her heart wanted to crawl up into a little ball and die yet again.

Son of a bitch. She didn't want to feel anything for the bastard. Not anymore.

She let the video play forward now, suddenly afraid she would lose them. But of course, she didn't. They just staggered down the hall to Nicole's room, Nicole shaking her dress a little and gesturing at her thighs. Dylan laughed and put his hand possessively on her back. That made her turn, and they kissed again, the same hot kiss they'd exchanged in the hallway downstairs, the kind that wrapped her around him. He took the keycard from her hand, and opened the door, backing her inside.

Serena caught the image of a red dress floating in the air before the door snaked closed.

Her heart split again. Her fist clenched. She wanted to put it through the screen, but she didn't. She started to stand, but a thought stopped her.

He had done something. Besides kissing Nicole, that is. He had done something else. Something—

Serena reversed the video, then watched, frame by frame. After Dylan took the keycard from Nicole, while she was wrapped around him, and he was holding her up with one hand (her back braced against the door), he used the keycard to open the door. And then, as her legs tightened around him, as her dress hiked up again, as he was probably even more entangled with her than he had been a second before, he slipped the keycard in his back pocket.

Cool and calculating, even in the middle of the hottest sex Serena had ever witnessed.

She watched it one more time to make certain. Yep, he had pocketed the keycard, and he would probably make a copy of it. She couldn't ever remember giving him her original key card, and he had gotten one from the desk when they moved to the suite, but a move like this would enable someone else to get into the room when Nicole and Dylan weren't there—if Dylan somehow made a copy.

Serena suspected he would make a copy as soon as Nicole was asleep.

Serena stood, suddenly reviewing every movement Dylan had made with her. One-handed, eyes closed, grabbing desktops and tables, and shoving things aside, telling her everything would be all right—yes, he had done so much more than one thing at a time.

That twisting in her heart had disappeared. That little maneuver of his made the last of the old naïve Serena die.

And she was glad of it.

Because she had only a few hours to put her plan into action.

TEN

First, the haircut. She hurried the hairdresser because she didn't want to get seen in the hallway. At some point, Dylan and Nicole would leave that room—sober, deciding to get married. Dylan seemed to like his women sober when he "married" them.

Serena had to watch carefully for that, because she still wasn't sure which chapel the substitute preacher was in.

While her hair was being cut, she had a full manicure, which she had done that trip two long years ago as well. It felt odd to pamper herself like this: she hadn't done it in a long time.

It didn't relax her. It made her feel like she was being primed for battle.

She finished, returned to her room, ordered room service, and hunkered down. She knew she wouldn't get a lot of sleep in the next twenty-four hours, and she was okay with that.

She could sleep after she was done with Dylan.

At six a.m., room service knocked on Nicole's door. Dylan answered, opening the door so that the waiter could take the food cart inside. Serena saw Nicole, wrapped in a fluffy robe, her feet bare, and her perfect hair so messy it was clear what she had been doing all night.

Dylan looked a lot more put together. How come Serena hadn't noticed that when they were together?

Dylan signed the tab for the food, which was odd, since he wasn't yet on the room. Maybe he had signed it to his room, or maybe the hotel didn't care.

Then the room service waiter pushed the cart out, leaving the tray with the food inside. As the waiter turned to head down the hall, the security cameras caught his face full-on.

It was the oniony man from the lobby. Serena gasped, the pieces of the scam coming together. Dylan hadn't done everything while Serena was asleep. He had merely collected the evidence and downloaded it or moved it or changed it. Then he had passed it off to an accomplice.

She and Dylan had room service every single day. She thought it was because they didn't want to get dressed, not because Dylan was feeding information to someone.

When the room service waiter arrived day after day, Serena had never gotten out of bed, too embarrassed to face the waiter. Nicole had gotten out of bed, but she looked a bit preoccupied. Still, Serena wondered if Nicole's presence had dampened Dylan's style.

Serena took a deep breath. Now, she knew the con was underway. Of course, she had known it last night, but she really knew it now. She had evidence to share with Kree, Castillo, and the FBI.

This was where Serena should have been a good girl. She could prevent a lot of heartache for Nicole right here.

But Serena wasn't about to prevent a few hours of heartache for one woman. Serena wanted to prevent heartache for an entire slew of women, all of whom would become victims if she didn't step in.

Oh, who was she kidding?

She wanted to destroy Dylan. She had always wanted to destroy Dylan. If she stepped in now, she would miss her chance.

He would get arrested either way; she was going to call the authorities eventually.

She just wanted a little payback first.

ELEVEN

Dylan and Nicole finally left the hotel room at one in the afternoon. Nicole was wearing a tasteful white lace dress with matching heels. She glowed, and Serena actually felt for her. Nicole had no idea what was coming.

Dylan wore a black suit, not silk, but tasteful, the kind an upper-middle-class man would bring on a business trip. He looked like a man who had never been married before—nervous, proud, happy.

He held Nicole's hand, then kissed it as the door to the room closed.

Serena could have scripted the next hour. Downstairs by elevator, although as Dylan wanted to kiss Nicole, she held him back: that woman wanted to look nice for her wedding photos. Dylan smiled, but Serena saw that his gaze had cooled just a little. He wanted the sexual mastery, not the pretty images.

The couple got out on the third floor of the hotel, which had a bridge to a variety of expensive stores. Serena tracked them to the most exclusive jewelry store in the shopping area. Outside, they clearly argued, but Dylan finally held sway. Serena knew his argument: *You only get married once*, he was saying, the bastard. *We need to do some things right. You'll wear this ring every single day of your life.*

Serena looked at her ring, glistening in the Vegas sunlight pouring in the window. She hadn't worn the ring every single day, but she would be lying if she said she hadn't thought about it—and him—day in and day out.

She made herself focus on the screen. Dylan and Nicole walked into the jewelry store, Dylan's hand possessively on the small of her back. Serena could almost feel that hand on the small of hers.

She made herself focus. She hadn't hacked into the security cameras of every jewelry store in the area, and she didn't think she should hack now. She waited, and watched, seeing only their forms through one of the corridor cameras.

It took longer than she had expected. She and Dylan had chosen within twenty minutes—eager, Serena thought, to get married and then back to their hotel room. But Nicole clearly wanted to find the perfect ring.

When they finally emerged, Dylan clutching a small bag with the store's logo, he looked a little frazzled. He hadn't enjoyed that last hour at all.

Nicole probably wasn't the kind of woman he could manipulate as easily as he manipulated Serena.

Nicole said something, and then he handed her the bag. She put it in her purse, and slipped her arm through his. They walked toward the lobby.

Serena prayed they would get a cab. If they got a cab, she could catch them. Him. The stupid substitute preacher.

She could bring an end to all of it.

She twisted her ring.

As they went through the lobby, Dylan stopped at the valet station, and handed one of the valets some cash. Serena felt her heart sink.

No cab. Somehow Dylan had a car.

Damn.

The couple went outside and waited, until a black SUV pulled up. The valet handed Dylan the keys, Dylan passed out more money, and Serena squinted for the license plate.

She didn't quite see it—at least, that was what she told herself.

She would wait until they returned. No matter where they went, it would only take a few hours at most.

She wouldn't take a nap, but she would rest. It was nearly showtime.

TWELVE

The SUV returned to the hotel at eight p.m., later than she expected. Serena had been going quietly insane. She worried that they were going to check out, that she'd never find them again, that they were onto her.

But the SUV pulled up, and as it stopped, Nicole got out, then glanced at her left hand, where a ring so big that Serena could see it on the security camera glistened.

Dylan came around the SUV, tossed his keys to the valet like a rich man would (or, more accurately, an asshole). Then the couple walked into the hotel, their steps perfectly in sync.

They stopped in the lobby, and Serena felt her heart clench. They were supposed to go to the most expensive bar in the place and toast their new marriage. That was what she had done—after Dylan had gotten them the honeymoon suite.

And the hotel staff had moved their belongings.

Serena let out a small breath.

Dylan turned, and walked to the desk—and Serena smiled.

Then she picked up her phone. She waited until Dylan and Nicole were done reserving a larger room, Nicole's high-heeled foot playing with the back of Dylan's leg the entire time. When they were done, they headed toward the restaurant complex, and Serena's smile grew.

She called Castillo first because, technically, it was Castillo's case.

"I'm here in Vegas at a conference," Serena lied, "and I think I just saw Dylan in my hotel."

"Don't go near him," Castillo said. "Where are you?"

Serena told her. Serena did not tell her that Dylan had already married and was heading to the bar.

Castillo could find that out for herself.

"You sit tight," Castillo said. "We'll handle this. And remember, he can't hurt you anymore."

She was so used to dealing with sexual assault victims. Serena remembered how her heart twisted when she watched that first kiss between Nicole and Dylan—and how it had taken Serena a while to get past that.

"I know he can't," Serena said, and that much was true. "Please, don't worry about me."

And then she hung up. She stared at the security cameras, saw Dylan and Nicole arguing in the corridor. This marriage wouldn't have lasted, even if it were real.

Dylan shrugged, then grinned, a look that Serena hadn't seen before.

Nicole led him—not to the bar, but to the fanciest restaurant in the place.

Clearly she wanted the full honeymoon package—the gorgeous ring, the fancy hotel suite, the pricey restaurant. She wanted the memories.

And, poor sap, she'd get them.

Serena waited until the couple followed the maître d' deep into the restaurant. Then she checked her appearance, added some lipstick, grabbed her purse, and headed downstairs.

THIRTEEN

Her heart was pounding—not with fear, but with anticipation. She wanted to do this. She wanted it almost as much as she had wanted Dylan that first night (hell, the entire time. Double hell, *still* wanted Dylan).

She strode across the hotel, and into the restaurant area. Men who already had a partner tried not to look at her. Men who were alone all smiled as if her appearance gave them hope she would go somewhere with them. Most women gave her the death stare, the one that told her they thought she looked prettier than they did. Other women openly flirted.

So she did look good.

Excellent. She needed to.

She clutched her purse to her side, and entered the restaurant. It smelled of garlic, roasting beef, and freshly baked bread. The maître d' tried to stop her. She gave him her widest smile.

"I'm meeting someone," she said, and pushed past him.

She saw Nicole first. They had a table in the corner. Nicole sat with her back to the wall, her beauty and happiness reflected in the discreet mirrors added just above the chairs to make the room seem bigger.

Dylan sat across from her, his suit coat open, his collar unbuttoned, and his tie loose. He looked like he had already had good sex. Maybe he had, in the car. Or maybe he got satisfied by a con well played.

He sat up as Serena approached, a frown on his face.

Serena made sure she wore a small smile, not a large one. She didn't want to look like the cat that swallowed the canary until all the feathers were in her mouth.

He set his napkin down, as if he were about to get out of the chair, when she reached him. She slipped her hands inside his suit, down his chest, feeling its familiarity, so flat and perfect. As she did that, she nibbled his ear, then worked her way down his neck, knowing what it did to him.

He gasped just a little, a sexual sound she had forgotten, and tried to move away, but she held him tightly.

"What are you doing?" Nicole demanded. "What's going on?"

Serena kept Dylan in his seat, pressing her breasts against his back, and unbuttoned the front of his shirt near his belt. He reached for her hands, but she slipped them against his warm skin.

She smiled, keeping her mouth against the fragrant side of Dylan's neck. "So this is the new one, Dylan?"

He started at the name.

"Oh, I'm sorry," she said, just a little louder. "I meant John. I forget what name he uses on these little excursions."

Nicole's face had gone white. She was looking at Dylan as if she expected him to say something.

The people at the nearby table were watching as well. A waiter, holding a silver ice bucket with a bottle of champagne inside, stood awkwardly by.

"Let me see the ring," Serena said as if she and Nicole were old friends. "He didn't make you buy it, did he? Sometimes he makes the woman buy, and I think that's so rude."

Dylan shoved at her. "Lady, you're crazy."

"I know, my love," she said, sliding her hands down further. He wasn't wearing underwear.

He grabbed her before she could touch his private parts. She could see his face in the mirror. He looked panicked.

Nicole's face had flushed. "Who *are* you?" she snapped at Serena.

"Oh, sweetie," Serena said. "He didn't explain, did he? I'm his wife. We were married years ago. Your marriage isn't legal. The document you signed isn't one that the State of Nevada recognizes, even if the ceremony were performed by a licensed preacher, which yours wasn't. That's just Dylan's—I mean John's—best friend."

"What?" Nicole asked.

"Oh," Serena said, her voice lowering. "Did you marry today? Am I early? You still had a few days of sex left, didn't you? Dylan likes his women to think it's legal. He says it makes them even hotter."

Serena lifted one of her hands and grabbed Dylan's chin tightly. He tried to open his mouth, but she turned his head toward her and kissed him, like she had wanted to kiss him since she saw him kiss Nicole.

Serena's other hand was still inside his pants. She could feel him respond.

She pulled her mouth away just enough to say, "My darling loves screwing women. I'm not always able to keep up with him, so I let him roam. Sometimes he gets a bit...involved—"

"I do not!" Dylan finally got some traction. He shoved her backwards. "You damn bitch! What do you think you're doing?"

Her heart was pounding. She hadn't expected him to get so furious.

He raised an arm and was about to hit her, when the waiter dropped the champagne bucket. It sloshed ice everywhere. One of the other diners stood and grabbed Dylan, who struggled against him, screaming obscenities at Serena.

"I'm done with you, you bitch. You have no right to be here! You're *done*."

Her mouth was dry, but she smiled anyway. "Not really. I'm just beginning. I'm going to follow you everywhere, and meet all of your wives. We'll have quite a coven, we wives of the con man named for a poet. We'll—"

"He's a con man?" Nicole was standing, clutching her purse to her chest. "You know he's a con man?"

Everyone looked at her. Water from the ice bucket was sliding across the floor, getting into her shoes, but she didn't even seem to notice.

"He tried to steal everything from me," Serena said.

"You could have *told* me," Nicole said, her voice thick with tears. "You could've stopped the wedding. You could've—"

"It wasn't legal," Serena said. "You're still single—"

Nicole let out a sob and launched herself across the table, pounding Dylan repeatedly with her fists. "You said you *loved* me, you *bastard*. You said—"

"He always says that." A new voice had entered the conversation. Kree stood behind the maître d', wearing an old brown polyester suit coat, and functional pants. She glared at Serena. "Detective Castillo told you to wait."

"And miss this?" Serena smiled. She felt positively giddy.

"It accomplishes nothing." Kree removed a pair of handcuffs from her belt. She expertly snapped the cuffs on Dylan, then dragged him away from the waiter.

"You have no right," Dylan said. "I've done nothing wrong."

Serena gasped at his audacity, but Nicole raised a high heel and kicked. Dylan turned slightly sideways, getting the point of the heel in his thigh.

His eyes narrowed as he glared at Nicole. "You were a hell of a lot more fun to screw than she was." He inclined his head at Serena. "I was looking forward to seeing what else you could do."

Nicole screeched and reached for him. Kree moved him even farther away.

Serena knew better than to say anything to Nicole. Serena recognized her pain. Instead, she ran a hand along Dylan's face.

"Oh, darling," she said. "You must be slipping. It really didn't take much to convince her that you're the scum of the earth."

His mouth opened in shock, and for a moment, she saw the real man underneath. Panicked, vulnerable, lost. Then his mouth closed and his face flushed. He pursed his lips, and she realized just in time that he was going to spit at her. She barely managed to dodge.

"How very third grade of you," she said. "A real man would apologize."

"For what? Giving you two the only fuck you've ever had?" he snapped.

Serena tilted her head. "Oh, Dylan, such ego. You were always a little too fast for me."

He made a growling sound, and Kree yanked him away from her. Another officer had shown up and was helping her.

Nicole had dissolved into a pile of tears. Two of the female patrons had their arms around her as she sobbed.

"I told you to wait." Castillo was standing near one of the tables, arms crossed.

"You sound like Detective Kree," Serena said. She tilted her head at Nicole. "You have a real victim there. You need to deal with her."

"And not the woman who went all vigilante on us?" Castillo's brown eyes missed nothing. She apparently saw the similar dress, the manicure, the haircut.

"I was just going to warn the new wife," Serena lied, "and I got carried away. I'll be happy to come to the station, though, and press charges."

"Tomorrow," Castillo said. "When I'm less pissed at you."

Serena smiled and picked her way out of the mess. Other officers and some security guards were huddled near the doorway. Dylan was being led away. He seemed small now, hunched, as if he'd lost something.

She almost wished she hadn't called the police. She hadn't had that much fun in years. Imagine what it would have been like to follow him from con to con, breaking it up at the exact right moment, having him look over his shoulder, always expecting her to ruin things.

She had planned this a bit too conservatively. She could have done that, and truly ruined him.

She sighed. Her giddiness was fading. She almost felt lost.

The police and the FBI would get enough information from Nicole to arrest the other team members. They'd find the oniony man and the substitute preacher and anyone else who was involved. The entire con would shut down.

The game was over. Serena had won.

She reached for her wedding ring, and started to slip it off. Then she looked at it, the way that Nicole had looked at hers when she got out of the SUV, with wonder and a bit of surprise that it was on her finger.

What was a wedding ring after all, but a trophy? The symbol of a woman who had truly tamed a man.

She closed her left hand into a fist, feeling stronger. Feeling powerful.

Feeling complete for the first time in her entire life.

She hadn't expected this happily ever after when she met Dylan.

But she would take it.

She would take it all.

THE WEDDING RING

THE ORIGINALLY PUBLISHED VERSION

ONE

T he smell of coffee woke her. Serena stretched her arm across the soft sheets to find Dylan's side of the bed cold. She eased her eyes open. He'd actually pulled the covers up, and placed them under the pillow.

She smiled. In the five days they'd been married, he hadn't done that before. She had teased him a lot about leaving the bed unmade.

His answer was serious at first: *We're in a hotel, babe. They make the bed for us.*

Then he slowly realized she was joking. *They would make the bed, babe,* he said, *if we ever leave it.*

And finally, he said, *I'll make the bed the minute I know we're not going to use it.*

Oddly, that last memory stabbed her heart. She sat up, covers pulled to her chest. The room wasn't as dark as it had been; light filtered in around the thick curtains.

She blinked. The smell of coffee was strong. She made herself take a deep breath and smile. Dylan was in the other room, with room service waiting for her. He probably hadn't wanted to wake her. He'd done that the last two days, telling her that she needed her strength.

And then he leered.

He had a good leer. She loved that leer, because of the twinkle in his eyes. He was the most handsome man she had ever seen— even after she had taken her beer goggles off.

She hadn't been drunk when she met him, but she hadn't been sober either. She'd been standing in one of the casino's beautifully decorated hallways, just outside the etched glass windows of the most popular nightclub in the place. She was wearing a slinky silver dress she had bought with her surprise slot winnings.

At the behest of the desk clerk when she checked in, she had taken one free pull on the gigantic slot machine in the lobby—and she'd won $10,000 instantly.

She was cautious with her cash, always had been. She had put $5,000 in an account in a major bank here in Vegas, planning to transfer all of it and close the account when she got home. The remaining money was found money that she added to her vacation stash.

And the first thing she had purchased had been a dress so slinky, she felt like another woman.

She drank like one too, a little something every night, hoping it would give her courage—or at least, make this two-week trip a bit more fun. The trip hadn't started as a single-woman adventure. Initially, she had booked it for herself and her boyfriend of long standing, Charles. When Charles ended their relationship three months before they were due to leave, she had kept the trip on the schedule because she felt like she had something to prove.

She called this trip the Liberation Vacation.

Three days in, she'd been feeling more restless than liberated. She was also feeling a bit pathetic. The alcohol helped just a little, but only a little. It led to her dancing by herself in a casino corridor because she wasn't certain she could face the flashing lights and blaring noise and ultimate shocking aloneness of dancing by herself inside that nightclub.

Then Dylan showed up—a blond god in a silk suit.

He was romance-novel gorgeous, broad shoulders, muscular torso, narrow hips, a body which she later learned was as perfect unclothed as it was clothed. His hair was trimmed just enough to be stylish, but not enough to make him look fussy. He had stuffed the tie in the pocket of his jacket, making him a little less perfect.

When he saw her, he had smiled at her, and extended his long-fingered hand. "A woman as pretty as you should never dance alone."

It had been a long time since someone called her pretty. Suddenly, the highlights she'd put in her hair, the weight she'd lost in the build-up to this Liberation Vacation, money she'd spent on the slinky dress she'd probably never wear at home were all worth it.

She took his hand, surprised and pleased to find calluses. He tucked her hand in the crook of his arm, and led her inside that nightclub. They'd danced and drank and laughed, and laughed, and laughed, and by the time they were done, their hands were all over each other.

She'd never been a public kisser, but she had been that night—hell, he could have taken her on the bar if he'd wanted to. In fact, she suggested it. He had said he didn't want them to get arrested at their magical first meeting.

After the nightclub closed, they ended up in his hotel room first, and barely made it through the door before the suit and the slinky dress came off. Combustible sex, of the kind she'd only read about, and then more sex, and some room service, and finally a bit of conversation, in which she learned that he was in Vegas to celebrate his own freedom—only his was a sad little freedom: his father had died two months earlier, and Dylan—he was Dylan Thomas, named for the Welsh poet—had been his father's caretaker for the past two years.

Freedom, and liberation, and the surprising loneliness.

Oh, clearly they had realized they were kindred souls. He was footloose now that the estate was settled, and she had to go back to work, and, he said, he loved Denver, had always meant to live there—and he'd give it a try for her. By the end of the day, that "try" had turned into a certainty, and the two of them knew they couldn't live without each other.

The Elvis Chapel was a cliché she wanted to avoid, but they both wanted to marry immediately, thinking it romantic. No plans, no preachers, no haggling over the bests. No china patterns, no wedding invitations, just them—him in his silk suit (which they had to have pressed) and she in her slinky dress, commemorating the moment of meeting.

He bought her roses and she bought him a matching boutonniere. They picked out expensive rings, with matching ruby stones and thick gold. He paid for hers, and she paid for his, and they clutched the boxes as they left the jewelry store, carefully located near some of the other chapels.

Only one chapel looked like a sedate place. At the edge of the Strip, where the rents were probably still cheap, the building was small and tasteful with soft organ music playing in the front, and a lovely little white and gold backdrop used for photographs.

A substitute preacher married them—the regular guy was on his own honeymoon (*Isn't that romantic?* the substitute asked with a comfortable smile)—and took a dozen photographs taken after Serena and Dylan filled out all of the various paperwork.

Her friends would hate it that she married Dylan so soon after meeting him, but while he paid the preacher, she texted them photos anyway, so they could see her joy as it happened. The photos covered everything: the chapel, Dylan from the side, the back, and then grinning at her as he walked up. The preacher gave them the actual wedding photos and a disk with the images so they could print out more copies.

Afterwards, they went back to Serena's hotel because her winnings had earned her an upgrade to one of the suites, and a conversation with the front desk clerk had gotten them yet another upgrade—a honeymoon suite, complete with champagne, caviar, chocolate-dipped strawberries, and two free room service meals.

Now, she followed the scent of coffee into the living room, after wrapping a robe around herself. The covered room service tray sat on the large table which she and Dylan had used for carnal purposes more than once.

There was no Dylan, and there was no note. She checked the bathroom. She frowned, wondering where he had gotten to, when her image in the mirror stopped her short.

Her lips were swollen, her cheeks scratched by stubble, her gold-streaked hair messy. She looked well and thoroughly satisfied.

She smiled at herself—and then the smile faded as she realized what was missing.

Dylan's toiletries.

He'd spread them across the vanity—the special shampoo for his gorgeous hair, the shaving cream for his ultra-sensitive (and oh, so lovely) skin, even his toothbrush. All missing.

Her heart skipped a beat, and she thought she misremembered where the toiletries had been, but she hadn't. She knew she hadn't.

Maybe he had put them in the half bath near the door—she had teased him enough about his "products," since he actually had more than she did. Maybe he was hiding them because she embarrassed him.

She pulled the robe tighter, and walked across the suite to the half bath near the door.

It looked lovely, with its little flower vase in one corner of the vanity, and the hotel toiletries on the other side. Who knew that the sight of a clean bathroom, beautifully decorated and absolutely perfect, would set her heart racing.

Racing and sinking at the same time.

She walked out of the little bathroom, her hands shaking now. Her body knew what her mind was refusing to acknowledge.

He wasn't here.

He had left.

But that wasn't possible. They loved each other. People who loved each other didn't treat each other like this. They didn't. They just didn't.

She walked quickly through the entire suite, suddenly angry that it was as large as the first apartment she had ever had. Lots of places to hide; lots of places to conceal things.

She looked in closets—empty except for her things. Her slinky little dress hung on a hanger, alone, not near his silk suit. He had said those two things should remain forever together.

Their wedding clothes.

Her dress. Alone.

She swallowed hard, kept looking. His suitcase was gone. His toiletries were gone. His clothes were gone.

The bed was made.

There was no note.

Except...

She stomped to the dining table, and lifted the lid off the room service tray.

One meal. Eggs, lightly scrambled. Toast, dark. A slice of watermelon. An uncut banana for later. And a pastry for dessert.

Just like she liked it.

And no note.

No damn note.

She flung the cover across the room. The cover clanged as it hit the wall, then clattered all the way to the floor. The sound was not satisfying.

Her lower lip trembled at the thought. That word: *Satisfied*. The bastard. The fucking bastard. Literally.

Her eyes teared up, and she took a deep breath.

She went back into the bedroom, and grabbed her phone, clicking it on, and froze.

It had reverted to factory settings. *He* had switched it to factory settings. All of her information was gone.

How had he gotten her password to unlock the phone?

And then she remembered him watching her as she opened her phone. Watching over and over again.

Her fingers shook, but she typed in all her information, then asked the phone to download her information from the cloud.

The phone told her that she did not have a cloud account. In fact, her phone told her she did not have any kind of account, and she had to sign up with a service provider.

She pulled the phone out of its case, saw the little scratch along the back that had been there since another case broke and her keys had defaced the phone's smooth surface.

It was her phone. But it didn't act like her phone.

She took a deep breath. It hitched. She took another, willing herself to remain steady.

Her purse sat on the chair near the window. She opened it. Her wallet was there, and so was the cash. Her driver's license—*I'll have to change that when I get back*, she had said with a laugh the night they married, when she decided to take his name. His name. Jesus. His name.

She refused to let her mind go any farther down that road. She had her driver's license, her credit cards, her insurance card, everything. But she stared at her wallet, afraid it would all bite her in ways she didn't understand.

She couldn't use her phone, but she could use the hotel's phone. In the closet, there was a phone book. She flipped the pages until she found hotels and casinos, kept flipping until she found his hotel, the one she had watched him check out of. But maybe he hadn't. Maybe he—

She called the front desk of that hotel, asked for Dylan Thomas, and waited as the clerk checked.

"I'm sorry, ma'am," the clerk said. "We do not have a guest by that name."

She tried her last name, then a variation of his name, then asked the clerk to see if someone was using the same credit card that Dylan had used when he stayed there about a week ago.

The clerk's tone got frosty. "Ma'am, I'm sorry. We don't give out that information."

"He's missing!" Serena said, her voice suddenly sounding like someone else's. Screechy and terrified and watery, and oh, so devastated. Was she devastated? She didn't want to be devastated. She couldn't be.

She had known him less than a week.

But she had married him.

The bastard.

"Oh, dear, ma'am," the clerk said and now her tone was sympathetic. "I'm afraid legally I can't just give this to someone over the phone, but we will work with the police on this. I hope you find him, ma'am. I'm sorry."

And then the clerk severed the connection.

Serena stared at the receiver as if the phone itself had caused Dylan to disappear. She made herself hang up. Hiccupping sobs threatened, but she wasn't going to allow them out.

She needed breakfast, but not the breakfast he had provided. She went back to the dining room table, grabbed the banana—the only thing that wouldn't have gotten cold or soggy—and then went to the bathroom with the gigantic shower.

She turned the water on scalding, stripped off the robe, and stepped inside, managing to control her mind until she lathered parts only a few other people had seen. Then she remembered the feel of Dylan's long fingers.

And that was when she started to scrub—not just to get the feel of him off her skin, but the memory of him out of her mind.

Forever.

Two

S he didn't feel better when she got out of the shower, but she felt different. Raw, aching. Determined.

She toweled off her hair, looked at herself in the mirror, and saw—not the satisfied woman from earlier—but someone new, someone with flushed skin and flat eyes, someone who had an expression of sheer fury, and the look of someone who could do actual damage with that fury.

In the shower, she had come up with a plan.

She needed to call the police first. She had the sinking feeling that Dylan had taken everything from her, so she couldn't rack up charges on the hotel phone.

Once the police were involved, then she would work with the hotel. After she got started on that, she would find out what happened to her phone.

She would check her accounts, and if he cleaned them out, which she expected (God, she was stupid—and no, she wouldn't let that thought loose too much or she'd collapse in a sobbing puddle of uselessness), *if he cleaned them out* (she thought loudly to herself, with emphasis, to control her emotional and unruly brain), she would pawn the damn wedding ring with its lovely stones that still glistened on her finger.

He had left all of her cash—five hundred dollars—which was something. Had he cared for her even a little bit? Or had he forgotten that she had cash?

She wiped her hand over her face. Emotions later. Situation first.

She sat on the hard living room couch, grabbed her mostly useless phone, and hit the emergency button. A keyboard showed up on screen, allowing her to call 911.

She did, and said, "I think I'm the victim of a terrible crime," and refused to burst into tears.

THREE

The police showed up fifteen minutes later. Two male officers and a female detective. The detective identified herself as Angela Castillo, part of the Las Vegas Sexual Assault Detail, which made Serena start. She hadn't reported a sexual assault.

She'd reported the marriage, the possible loss of everything, his disappearance, but not—

And then she flushed.

When looked at from a legal perspective, if he had no intention of staying married to her, then—

She excused herself, went to the pristine small bathroom, and threw up.

Castillo stood in the doorway. She was in her forties, in shape, with caramel colored skin and dark eyes that seemed to miss nothing. She waited until Serena had cleaned herself up before saying,

"Come on. Let's talk alone. Where would you be the most comfortable?"

Suddenly Serena wasn't comfortable anywhere. The whole

hotel room was the scene of the crime. The whole damn city was the scene of the crime.

Castillo looked at the officers. "Just give us a minute."

"No," Serena said. "We have to find him before he gets away."

"You don't know when he left?" Castillo asked.

Serena shook her head.

"Okay, a description, then, and his name. We can start there."

Serena gave his name, and his description to the officers. "I have a picture on my..." and then her voice trailed off. Her phone had been wiped clean. "Maybe with the papers?"

She had put the wedding certificate in her suitcase. She walked to the closet she'd been using, opened the suitcase, and the documents—which had been in a folder on top—were still there. She hadn't put them in the little pouch underneath where she usually put important information while traveling. She had been proud of that damn marriage certificate. She had looked at it whenever she opened the suitcase.

She pulled out the folder, opened it, saw the certificate remained, but there were no pictures any longer—at least not of him. One of her, the only one alone, *the bride shot,* the preacher had called it. She stood before the gold altar in her slinky dress, clutching the roses. She had looked pretty and happy and hopeful.

Naïve little idiot that she had been.

Serena swallowed. "He took them. All of them. Pictures and everything."

"Let me see." Castillo had slipped on gloves. She reached for the folder.

Castillo didn't look at the photo, but at the marriage certificate. Then she showed it to the officers who were also in the room.

"This isn't a valid marriage license." Castillo looked at the officers. "We're going to need someone from Financial and Property Crimes ASAP. Tell the captain we need—oh, never mind. I'll call it in. You go down to the desk, ask to get copies of all of the security video for this floor for the last week, and this morning's video as well. See if we get a good image of this guy."

The officers nodded, and then walked out of the room.

"Let's sit in the living room." Castillo was holding the folder with its one pathetic photograph, clearly waiting for Serena to make a decision.

Serena nodded, then followed Castillo to that hard couch. A sexual assault victim? But she'd given her consent. Over and over. And the sex had been good. It hadn't been coerced.

But it hadn't been what she thought either. It hadn't been the celebration of two people in love, two people who had found each other despite the odds.

She frowned and rubbed her hands on her knees, feeling an ache throughout her body.

Dylan had violated her. Not sexually, not really. She would have wanted him, even for that one-night stand.

But he had violated her emotionally. Intellectually. Personally.

In every single way that counted.

Now, these revelations were taking her heart and crushing it, one little piece at a time.

FOUR

T he next few days were a blur of interviews, explanations, and bureaucratic horrors. Dylan had emptied her bank accounts, taken cash advances from her credit cards at the hotel casino—where she had identified him as her husband on that giddy first night (and every night thereafter). He had taken an online second mortgage against her house.

Serena's house sitter had stopped a stranger from letting himself in—with Serena's keys—so that he could help himself to her belongings. The stranger had looked nothing like Dylan. *Believe me*, Serena's sitter said. *I would have remembered a handsome blond. This guy was short and dumpy and smelled of onions.*

Dylan had taken the sim card from Serena's phone, replacing the card with another. He hadn't wiped the memory as much as stolen everything about the phone that made it Serena's.

Except he hadn't known about the automatic cloud backup. Once the helpful man at the cellular store had helped Serena reset her phone, the cloud downloaded, with a few extra treasures.

Photographs of Dylan, not the ones in the memory—he had

clearly deleted those at night while she slept—but buried in the texts she had sent her friends. She had forgotten about those, and told Castillo about them.

The detective Castillo had brought in from Financial and Property Crimes, a hard-faced woman named Kree, had asked for permission to dig through the phone. The phone was where Dylan had gained most of his access. He had everything of Serena's, from her social security number to her passwords, neatly stored in a little unmarked book which she had shown him, a book she kept in her carry-on (with another copy at home).

He had emptied her accounts the day he left, but the other things— the second mortgage, the new credit cards in her name, the credit lines he had opened with her very stellar credit number —those had all happened while she slept, sated, from their lovemaking.

Castillo had looked at Serena with empathy. Kree had looked at her with hard-edged pity. Serena had the sense before the end of the first day that Kree believed most financial crime victims got exactly what they deserved.

But Kree was efficient and helpful. She got the new credit lines and second mortgage cancelled, got the various banks to absorb all of the losses except the important ones—at least to Serena. The actual cash he had taken from her accounts he had done with her written permission, using the signature she had stored in her phone, and he had done so while she thought she was still married to him.

At Kree's advice, Serena consulted with an attorney (one free hour, thankfully) and the attorney said that withdrawing permission after a major fraud had occurred was often hard. Especially since Serena had been in Dylan's company when the fraud happened. The banks would probably sue on that one, the attorney had said, and while they wouldn't win, they would tie her up in court.

Much as this attorney wanted to represent her, he said, she would be better off writing off the losses and beginning again.

His words were harsh; his manner hadn't been. In fact, he had apologized several times, as if he were personally responsible for Dylan's actions.

Everyone was kind to her, and with the exception of Kree, treated her like Dylan had broken her.

Serena was beginning to like Kree more and more. Kree didn't care about Serena's emotional state. Kree wanted to put Dylan away.

"This con is incredibly organized," Kree said one afternoon when Castillo wasn't in the room. "This Dylan guy had a team. The substitute preacher, the guy at your house. I'm sure there were others. And they targeted you and played you. They've done this before. Just not in Vegas."

"I—I'm the first?"

"Here, it seems," Kree said. "We can't find any evidence of this happening to someone else. I have an associate reaching out to the hotels to see if someone reported something like this to them, but the hotels should call us if they realize that a major fraud ring is working the city."

"Maybe the women involved didn't report it," Serena said, trying not to wrap her arms around her torso. She'd been doing that a lot lately. "It's pretty embarrassing. I mean, who would think—"

"Do you know how many people elope in Vegas with someone they just met?" Kree gave her that flat stare. "Enough so that at any given time, there are at least fifty wedding chapels in this city. Fifty. A good half of the weddings here are between drunks who just met."

"Thanks," Serena muttered, knowing Kree believed Serena fit that description. She didn't want to correct Kree's misperception. Serena hadn't been drunk at her wedding—at least with alcohol.

"That's what's bothering me," Kree said, ignoring Serena's slide into self-pity (which Serena liked; it was enabling her to ignore her slide too). "With this many wedding chapels, and so many lonely whatever-happens-in-Vegas-stays-in-Vegas women coming every single day, we should have encountered this crew before. And we haven't."

"If they're not local, how did they get the chapel?" Serena asked.

"He really was a substitute preacher, hired for two weeks while the regular guy went on vacation," Kree said. "Of course, all of the substitute's information was false. It went deep enough that a cursory background check would have seemed on the up-and-up."

"So everyone there—?"

"The regular organist was sick that night," Kree said. "Severe food poisoning, which she got two days into the substitute preacher's gig."

"You think he did it," Serena said.

Kree nodded. "Like I said. Organized. We're bringing in the FBI on this. They have a crackerjack financial fraud team, and since this ring crossed state lines by going after your Denver house, they'll be handling a lot of the case."

"You're not?" Serena felt like she was losing her lifeline.

For the first time, Kree smiled at her. "I'm sticking on this one, whether the feebies like it or not. What these guys did to you..."

Kree shook her head, then bit her lower lip. Her entire body was rigid with fury.

"What those guys did to you," Kree said after a moment in which she took control of her voice, "that was personal. Getting to know you, *seducing* you. They didn't just steal the identity of a name on a credit card. They took your identity, made you volunteer to get a new name, and let you think you were walking into the sunset with the man of your dreams. They're not in this for the money. They're in it to destroy their marks. *That's* unacceptable. We have to catch them before they do it again."

Serena's throat had gone dry. She had to swallow three times before she could speak.

"They didn't destroy me," she said, but her voice sounded almost like a whisper. Broken. Ruined.

Kree looked at her.

Serena swallowed again. "They *didn't*. I'm right here. And I'm going to destroy them right back."

FIVE

T he first thing Serena did upon return from the police station was move to a different room. The hotel comped it, as if they were responsible for Dylan.

The new room was in a different wing, with different décor. She still had a suite, but it looked nothing like the old suite, and she was grateful for that. She had moved her own suitcase, after the police were done with it, and as she hung up her clothes, making the room one-hundred-percent hers, her fingers ran across the almost-invisible zipper beneath her clothes.

The pouch where she stored her important papers while she was in a hotel room. She always removed them and put them in her purse when she got on a plane, but otherwise she left them here.

She hadn't expected to be robbed by her own husband.

Serena took a deep calming breath, something that still wasn't habit yet, and made herself open the pouch.

The documents for her new money market account—the one she had set up for taxes and incidentals from her win the day she arrived—were still inside. Her fingers lingered over them. She hadn't told Dylan about this account. She had told him that she had saved some of the money for taxes, and they could spend the rest, but she hadn't told him she had started a new account to hold that money separate from everything else.

She would have told him, but it had slipped her mind. *He* had made it slip her mind.

She smiled, feeling the first ray of hope in days.

She grabbed her phone to check the account, then realized she hadn't set up online banking for that account. Instead, she called the bank using its 800-number, that old system which felt so 20th century now.

After she punched in more numbers than she cared to think about, she discovered a piece of information that made her giddy: She still had the full $5,000 of her winnings.

She suddenly didn't feel broke any more.

She certainly had less money than she'd had when she fake-married Dylan, but she wasn't going to live paycheck-to-paycheck, like she had feared.

She let out a shuddery sigh and sank down on a nearby chair. Dylan hadn't taken *everything*, the damn bastard.

That realization gave her an odd feeling of power. He hadn't entirely outsmarted her. He wasn't totally brilliant. He could be defeated.

She could defeat him.

She just had to figure out how.

SIX

Her first order of business was to put her life back together. Which sounded easier than it actually was. After the police finished with her, after she found a legal counselor and a financial advisor and a fraud specialist who was going to help her repair the damage that Dylan had done, she had to leave Las Vegas.

She was happy to do so. More than happy.

But her home, a Victorian on a twisted street in historic Denver, didn't feel like home any longer. It felt like it belonged to another woman—and essentially, it did.

Serena sold the house quickly and for a good price. Instead of putting all of the money in the bank in an account someone could break into, she scattered it through a variety of investments, none she tracked on her phone. She bought a luxury condo in downtown Denver, on the upper floors of one of the luxury hotels, figuring if she decided to leave the city, she could rent the damn place out.

The condo looked nothing like her old house. The condo was modern, with white walls and spectacular city views, stainless steel appliances, and interior bedrooms that had a whiff of hotel design to them. She didn't care. She dumped her old furniture, bought new for the condo, and added some modern art, something the old her would have hated. But she liked the jagged edges and the bright bold colors.

She upgraded her wardrobe too, trendy items, as trendy as her condo, and as brightly colored as the paintings. She took night classes in computers, learning the ins and outs of the internet, occasionally cringing at all of the mistakes she had made with her privacy B.D.

Before Dylan. Before Disaster. Before Deciding to change.

She was going to quit her job soon, but no one knew that except her. She had to struggle to pay attention to the classics. She wasn't a professor anymore. She didn't care if the little idiots learned anything.

Her friends were trying to slow her down. They complained when she sold the house. They complained when she moved. They complained when she cut her hair. They complained when she got new clothes.

When they complained too much, she stopped calling them. She wanted to say she made new friends, but she really didn't. She made new acquaintances, people she could laugh with in the bars near her condo, people whom she watched get drunk while she stayed startlingly sober. She learned to sip her wine—no more guzzling beer, no more mixed drinks, no more nothing—and she learned to watch.

She saw pickpockets, working girls, and escorts. She saw the scammers and the flimflam artists. And she realized just how rare Dylan had been.

Usually women ran his kind of scam—not the marrying part,

but the sex part. Using desire to get not just in someone's pants but into their wallets as well. Most of the women did it in one night, and many of them got arrested.

No one, as far as she could tell, ever managed to marry and scam—except those men who had different wives in different states, something she slowly learned was a different pathology altogether.

She made a study of con artists and bar behavior. When she wasn't watching people, she explored the internet, searching for a familiar face, searching for a pattern.

One after another, her counselors fired her. *You don't seem to want to get better*, one said to her.

I didn't know I was ill, Serena said in return.

You have no desire to explore your own healing, another counselor said.

I've repaired my life, Serena answered.

No, the counselor said. *You* changed *your life. That's not the same thing.*

Serena hadn't argued the point, although she could have. *She* hadn't changed her life. Dylan had. From the moment she met him. The fantastic sex (which she still sometimes dreamed about), the fake marriage, the hopes for the future—all came about because she met Dylan. That this particular happily-ever-after ended with the princess getting screwed royally by someone posing as Prince Charming didn't alter the fact that the chance meeting in the corridor outside the nightclub would have changed Serena's life no matter what.

She kept hiring counselors, though, mostly as someone to talk to. On her eighth counselor, she finally figured out how to use the system. She talked sideways about Dylan, about what kind of personality he had to have, about what made him tick.

If she figured out how what kind of person he was, she lied to the counselor, she would heal.

This particular counselor bought the argument for exactly two sessions. The next counselor for three. The next for another two. They argued that her healing had nothing to do with Dylan, and she privately begged to differ.

As they spent the hours she paid for analyzing him, she learned a few things.

She didn't believe the counselors who sympathetically said he had probably been sexually abused as a child or that he had a pathological hatred of women. She'd met a few men who hated women. It always came out sideways.

The counselors she believed were the ones who called him a sociopath. He had the charm and the charisma, the lack of interest in society's rules, and the love of putting something over on others.

He clearly had done that with her.

The problem was that people like Dylan felt no remorse, guilt, or shame. They blamed others when caught. So all of the FBI's work in finding him, all of the work Kree was doing and keeping Serena apprised of, wouldn't devastate Dylan, even if he was arrested. He'd be disappointed, but he'd blame all of them for his situation, not himself.

Sociopaths, one counselor said to Serena, *are all about control.*

And that, that little sentence, that one small idea, reverberated through her head for weeks.

Control. She had ceded control to him, and he had taken control of everything else.

But he had made it a game. From the name, to the sex, to the pretend marriage.

It had all been a game.

And games were all about winners and losers.

After she had that realization, her smiles became real, and her determination became strong.

She dropped the counselors and made finding Dylan her number one priority.

SEVEN

I t took nearly two years and a lot of focus. Even then, she wasn't certain she had found the right crew.

She used the information she got from the authorities, but she never gave them any information in return. The FBI had found a pattern—the crew would hit an area, usually with a casino, but not always; usually with a great nightlife, but not always; sometimes with relatively simple marriage license requirements, but not always.

The reports were fewer than reports on most fraud crews, because of the thing that Serena had said: women were often embarrassed to admit they had been taken. Some even hired a divorce attorney only to learn that they hadn't really been married in the first place.

The FBI searched for a pattern, Kree watched for the crew's return to Vegas (while keeping Serena apprised) and Serena employed increasingly more sophisticated facial recognition software as she searched likely areas.

She hooked up with a hacker group online, learned how to get into hotel security cameras, and make traffic cameras near hot spots do her bidding.

The FBI made a map of where the crew had been, and Kree had forwarded it. Serena looked at the pattern and did exactly what the authorities did: she tried to figure out where the crew would go next.

But the authorities had to wait for a crime.

She didn't.

And she had the benefit of knowing not just what Dylan looked like, but how he moved, how he slid through a crowd, how he touched women. She also knew what the substitute preacher looked like.

But that didn't find Dylan for her.

Three patterns did.

In the towns without overnight wedding chapels like Vegas, the substitute preacher set up a website for his marriage services, and attached it, like a barnacle, to the regular county clerk's office site. When engaged couples figured out that they wanted to marry, the website would send them to the preacher to set up his bona fides. It took a little time, but this crew seemed to have nothing but time.

That, combined with the travel pattern the FBI figured out, helped her find the preacher.

But it was Dylan's ego that helped her find him.

He assumed he was smarter than everyone else, prettier, smoother, better educated. In one town, he was Bob Browning. In another, Edward Cummings. And with Serena, he had been Dylan Thomas.

Famous male poets—Robert Browning, e. e. cummings, Dylan Thomas.

If the mark knew the name, like she had, Dylan copped to it—

my parents named me for the poet. If the mark didn't, no one said a word.

And no one else had noticed, except her.

She kept a list of poet names, and had various online alerts set up so that she could track the arrival/appearance of one of those names in the systems of the hotels in the locales that should've been next on the list.

The crew had a system that the FBI found. The crew would go to one city per state, never more than one in a trip, and never to adjoining states. So after they had left Serena in Las Vegas, they went to Washington State. They never visited the same state in the same year, but they seemed to have favorite states, Nevada being one of them.

Two years, which meant they were due. And after they left Florida, Serena knew they would start all over again. They always went west to east, never east to west. They would skip California, because they always seemed to skip California, which was leading the FBI to believe that the crew had history there, history that probably meant they didn't want to do anything to alert the California authorities.

The FBI was investigating that angle, or so Kree said, but they had little to go on. Serena didn't care about that angle. She cared about catching the crew in the act.

She had a plan.

And when a blond, exceedingly handsome John Donne checked into the priciest hotel on the Las Vegas strip, she knew she had found him.

EIGHT

Serena did not tell Kree or Castillo that she was returning to Las Vegas. She simply arrived. On the flight from Denver, she watched the hotel's security footage over and over again. She hadn't needed her special illegal facial recognition software to recognize Dylan. She knew every inch of that face, and even after she had cleaned up the security footage, she knew that his appearance hadn't changed at all.

Hers had. She was thin to the point of bony, her hair darker and longer. She no longer fit into the slinky dress (yes, she'd kept it), and her wedding ring (yes, she'd kept that too) spun on her left finger.

She'd wrapped yarn around the back of the ring as if she were a teenager, but after she'd checked into a different megahotel across South Las Vegas Boulevard from Dylan's, she scouted hair boutiques so that she could get hers wedge-cut and lightened. She didn't do it immediately—she didn't want Dylan to recognize her (even though she doubted he would)—but she did buy another slinky dress. It wasn't quite the same as the original, but it was close.

Serena had the same shoes, however. She could reappear as her old self at any point. "Old self" wasn't quite accurate: she had only been that slinky blond self for six days, six marvelous delusional days when she thought the fairy tale would never end.

She had no idea how Dylan picked his marks, although she had a theory. She had won that jackpot at the beginning of her stay two years ago, and babbled to the hotel staff like an idiot about the Liberation Vacation and how it was starting perfectly.

Over the years she (and the FBI and Kree) all doubted that Dylan had a crew member on staff, so that meant that he watched for some lucky hapless woman to reveal her loneliness in a painful and public fashion.

He had to spend his days watching for her.

Serena set up a wireless station inside her hotel room, so she didn't have to use the hotel's creaky old system. And she watched the lobby for a few hours before realizing that Dylan wasn't down there, but someone else was.

A short, dumpy guy who looked like he might actually smell of onions moved around the lobby, monkeying with his phone, sitting in a chair, going in and out of the nearby hotel gift shop. Serena didn't know for certain because she had never seen him before, but she was pretty sure that the man she was watching was the same one who had let himself into her house two years before, using her own keys.

He finally left the lobby about four hours in, and it didn't look like anyone had replaced him. Which meant he'd found the right mark.

She reviewed the footage, wishing she had audio as well as video. People—especially nervous people—revealed too much when they were checking into hotels.

She ended up with three possibles—all not-quite-pudgy blondes who looked both lonely and nervous—and watched the dumpy guy's reaction to them. He kept his eye on one for a tad too long. Serena was going to go with her, until she realized that he wasn't looking at the pudgy lonely woman. He was looking at a willowy blonde who seemed ever-so-slightly angry.

The willowy blonde smiled and laughed as she checked in, but the desk clerk looked a bit uncomfortable, the way people did when they heard too much information about someone they didn't know. Then the blonde held out a sparkling diamond ring, shook it at the clerk, and laughed again.

The clerk shrugged, took out a map, and circled someplace on it.

Serena's breath caught. She would bet her last dollar that the blonde wanted to sell that ring. Not pawn it. Sell it.

The crew wasn't targeting lonely women. They were targeting *angry* women traveling alone. After all, what had Serena and her Liberation Vacation been if not angry? She had just been too repressed to admit it by using words like "anger" and "furious." Instead, she had made jokes about her trip.

Serena hacked into the hotel's system, saw that the blonde— one Nicole Warrington—had checked into a suite that had been booked months before, and knew, knew, she was looking at Dylan's next "wife."

If Serena was still a good little girl, she would have called Kree and Castillo and alerted them. But she wasn't. Kree and Castillo would screw everything up.

If they asked later, Serena would say that she wasn't certain what happened to Dylan after she saw him check in.

And if she was honest with herself, she wondered why he was in the same hotel as the mark.

Or maybe he wasn't. Maybe he had gotten the room as insurance, let the dumpy guy use it, and had also gotten another room at a different hotel. That other room would also be under the name John Donne—if, indeed, he was running the same scam.

She would search for that in the morning. Just like she would try—again—to search wedding chapel "pastors." That was harder. Even though the chapels had online advertising, their websites were mostly static, and their business was in-person, so she couldn't figure out if they had hired someone new or gotten a substitute preacher.

She knew that Kree monitored the original wedding chapel, but Serena doubted the crew would use the same chapel twice.

She stayed in her room, ordered room service, and watched security footage until she saw Nicole Warrington leave her suite in a gorgeous red designer gown that showed every single curve to great advantage.

Nicole Warrington looked like a woman trying to shake off a man any way she possibly could.

For several heart-stopping minutes, Serena worried that Nicole would go to a nightclub outside of the massive hotel/casino complex.

But her worries faded as Nicole marched down to the most expensive nightclub inside the complex. Dylan would have to work quickly to catch this woman, because other men would be lined up.

Serena hoped he would work the corridor again, because seeing what he was doing inside the nightclub would be hard. The place had security, but it also had dim lighting that was punctuated by strobe lights when the music demanded it, and she would have trouble seeing faces.

Nicole Warrington went inside, and Serena didn't see Dylan at all.

She let out a breath, wondering if she had focused on the wrong mark.

She didn't want to miss this opportunity, and she was afraid that she might.

NINE

There was only one real exit to the club, which Serena monitored for four hours. While she watched, she worked on a second screen, searching lower-tier hotels for John Donne. She almost missed him. Facial recognition didn't find him, because he wore a ball cap low over his face, and he didn't register as John Donne.

He registered as Jonathon Donne.

The thing that confirmed it for her, though, was as she watched the security footage, she saw him roll the keycard over his fingers, just like a poker player rolled a card. He had done that with their keycard more than once.

She knew now that she was on the clock.

She had started reviewing the front desk footage for the mega-hotel when Nicole Warrington staggered out of the nightclub. Serena let out a breath. She had forgotten: the mark had to be drunk or at least tipsy before Dylan would approach.

And then he walked out, perfect in a gray suit that shimmered in the soft light. Nicole saw him, laughed, and extended her hand. Then they exchanged a kiss that Serena could almost taste.

At the moment, it looked like Nicole was in charge, not Dylan. He looked like the perfect goofy pickup, the guy who couldn't believe his luck. They kissed again, and she slid her hands under his suit coat.

A hotel security guard tapped him on the shoulder, and clearly told them to get a room.

They laughed, and staggered away. They headed to her room, which surprised Serena. Dylan had convinced Serena to go to his, although she couldn't remember how. Maybe she had balked at bringing him to hers. She probably had, with her old paranoia about being robbed.

Not that anyone was thinking of robbery at that moment, except maybe Dylan. He had his back against the row of mirrors inside the elevator, and Nicole was pressed against him.

Serena had to get up and walk away from the computer, her entire body shaking.

She had just become jealous. This wouldn't work if she were jealous. Dammit, she still had feelings for that man, buried deep, but not as deep as she thought.

Serena made herself breathe. Dylan was not her husband. He wasn't even named Dylan. He was some man, some horrible man, who had just targeted another vulnerable drunken woman.

Serena sat back down and reversed the video just a bit. She froze the frame on Dylan's face and made herself stare at it.

This is the face of a man who exchanges sex for money, she reminded herself, mouthing the words as she thought them. *This is the expression of a man who gets off on using people for his own purposes. The excitement of screwing a mark meant more to him than the sex act itself.*

She let the video play forward now, suddenly afraid she would lose them. But of course, she didn't. They just staggered down the hall to Nicole's room, Nicole shaking her dress a little. Dylan laughed. That made her turn, and they kissed again, the same hot kiss they'd exchanged in the hallway downstairs, the kind that wrapped her around him. He took the keycard from her hand, and opened the door, backing her inside.

Serena caught the image of a red dress floating in the air before the door snaked closed.

Her heart split again. She started to stand, but a thought stopped her.

He had done something. Besides kissing Nicole, that is. He had done something else. Something—

Serena reversed the video, then watched, frame by frame. After Dylan took the keycard from Nicole, while she was wrapped around him, and he was holding her up with one hand, he used the keycard to open the door. And then, as her legs tightened around him, as her dress hiked up, he slipped the keycard in his back pocket.

Cool and calculating.

Serena watched the video one more time to make certain. Yep, he had pocketed the keycard, and he would probably make a copy of it. Serena couldn't ever remember giving him her original key card, and he had gotten one from the desk when they moved to the suite, but a move like this would enable someone else to get into the room when Nicole and Dylan weren't there.

Serena suspected he would make a copy as soon as Nicole was asleep.

That twisting in her heart had disappeared. That little maneuver of his made the last of the old naïve Serena die.

And she was glad of it.

Because she had only a few hours to put her plan into action.

TEN

First, the haircut. She hurried the hairdresser because she didn't want to get seen in the hallway. At some point, Dylan and Nicole would leave that room—sober, deciding to get married. Dylan seemed to like his women sober when he "married" them.

Serena had to watch carefully for that, because she still wasn't sure which chapel the substitute preacher was in.

While her hair was being cut, she had a full manicure, which she had done on that trip two long years ago as well. It felt odd to pamper herself like this: she hadn't done it in a long time.

It didn't relax her. It made her feel like she was being primed for battle.

She finished, returned to her room, ordered room service, and hunkered down. She knew she wouldn't get a lot of sleep in the next twenty-four hours, and she was okay with that.

She could sleep after she was done with Dylan.

At six a.m., room service knocked on Nicole's door. Dylan

answered, opening the door so that the waiter could take the food cart inside. Nicole, wrapped in a fluffy robe, her perfect hair messy, was barely visible.

Dylan looked a lot more put together. He signed the tab for the food, which was odd, since he wasn't yet on the room. Maybe he had signed it to his room, or maybe the hotel didn't care.

Then the room service waiter pushed the cart out, leaving the tray with the food inside. As the waiter turned to head down the hall, the security cameras caught his face full-on.

It was the oniony man from the lobby. Serena gasped, the pieces of the scam coming together. Dylan hadn't done everything while Serena was asleep. He had merely collected the evidence and downloaded it or moved it or changed it. Then he had passed it off to an accomplice.

She and Dylan had room service every single day. She thought it was because they didn't want to get dressed, not because Dylan was feeding information to someone.

When the room service waiter arrived day after day, Serena had never gotten out of bed, too embarrassed to face the waiter. Nicole had gotten out of bed, but she looked a bit preoccupied. Still, Serena wondered if Nicole's presence had dampened Dylan's style.

Serena took a deep breath. Now, she knew the con was underway. Of course, she had known it last night, but she really knew it now. She had evidence to share with Kree, Castillo, and the FBI.

This was where Serena should have been a good girl. She could prevent a lot of heartache for Nicole right here.

But Serena didn't want to prevent a few hours of heartache for one woman. Serena wanted to prevent heartache for an entire slew of women, all of whom would become victims if she didn't step in.

Oh, who was she kidding?

She wanted to destroy Dylan. She had always wanted to destroy Dylan. If she stepped in now, she would miss her chance.

He would get arrested either way; she was going to call the authorities eventually.

She just wanted a little payback first.

ELEVEN

Dylan and Nicole finally left the hotel room at one in the afternoon. Nicole was wearing a tasteful white lace dress with matching heels. She glowed, and Serena actually felt for her. Nicole had no idea what was coming.

Dylan wore a black suit, not silk, but tasteful, the kind an upper-middle-class man would bring on a business trip. He looked like a man who had never been married before—nervous, proud, happy.

He held Nicole's hand, then kissed it as the door to the room closed.

Serena could have scripted the next hour. Downstairs by elevator, although Dylan wanted to kiss Nicole, she held him back: that woman wanted to look nice for her wedding photos. Dylan smiled, but Serena saw that his gaze had cooled just a little. He wanted the sexual mastery, not the pretty images.

The couple got out on the third floor of the hotel, which had a bridge to a variety of expensive stores. Serena tracked them to the most exclusive jewelry store in the shopping area. Outside, they clearly argued, but Dylan finally held sway. Serena knew his argument: *You only get married once*, he was saying, the bastard. *We need to do some things right. You'll wear this ring every single day of your life.*

Serena looked at her ring, glistening in the Vegas sunlight pouring in the window. She hadn't worn the ring every single day, but she would be lying if she said she hadn't thought about it— and him—day in and day out.

She made herself focus on the screen. Dylan and Nicole walked into the jewelry store, Dylan's hand possessively on the small of her back. Serena could almost feel that hand on the small of hers.

It took longer than she had expected. She and Dylan had chosen within twenty minutes—eager, Serena thought, to get married and then back to their hotel room. But Nicole clearly wanted to find the perfect ring.

When they finally emerged, Dylan clutching a small bag with the store's logo, he looked a little frazzled. He hadn't enjoyed that last hour at all.

Nicole probably wasn't the kind of woman he could manipulate as easily as he'd manipulated Serena.

Nicole said something, and then he handed her the bag. She put it in her purse, and slipped her arm through his. They walked toward the lobby.

Serena prayed they would get a cab. If they got a cab, she could catch them. Him. The stupid substitute preacher.

She could bring an end to all of it.

She twisted her ring.

As they went through the lobby, Dylan stopped at the valet station, and handed one of the valets some cash. Serena felt her heart sink.

No cab. Somehow Dylan had a car.

Damn.

The couple went outside and waited, until a black SUV pulled up. The valet handed Dylan the keys, Dylan passed out more money, and Serena squinted for the license plate.

She didn't quite see it.

She would have to wait until they returned. No matter where they went, it would only take a few hours at most.

She wouldn't take a nap, but she would rest. It was nearly showtime.

TWELVE

The SUV returned to the hotel at eight p.m., later than she expected. Serena had been going quietly insane. She worried that they were going to check out, that she'd never find them again, that they were onto her.

But the SUV pulled up, and as it stopped, Nicole got out, a huge ring on her left hand glistening in the security camera.

Dylan came around the SUV, tossed his keys to the valet like a rich man would. Then the couple walked into the hotel, their steps perfectly in sync.

They stopped in the lobby, and Serena felt her breath catch. They were supposed to go to the most expensive bar in the place and toast their new marriage. That was what she had done—after Dylan had gotten them the honeymoon suite.

As the hotel staff had moved their belongings.

Serena let out a small breath.

Dylan turned, and walked to the desk—and Serena smiled.

Then she picked up her phone. She waited until Dylan and

Nicole were done reserving a larger room, Nicole's high-heeled foot playing with the back of Dylan's leg the entire time. When they were done, they headed toward the bar and restaurant complex, and Serena's smile grew.

She called Castillo first because, technically, it was Castillo's case.

"I'm here in Vegas at a conference," Serena lied, "and I think I just saw Dylan in my hotel."

"Don't go near him," Castillo said. "Where are you?"

Serena told her. Serena did not tell her that Dylan had already married and was heading to the bar.

Castillo could find that out for herself.

"You sit tight," Castillo said. "We'll handle this. And remember, he can't hurt you any more."

She was so used to dealing with sexual assault victims. Serena remembered how her heart twisted when she watched that first kiss between Nicole and Dylan—and how it had taken Serena a while to get past that.

"I know he can't," Serena said, and that much was true. "Please, don't worry about me."

And then she hung up. She stared at the security cameras, saw Dylan and Nicole arguing in the corridor. This marriage wouldn't have lasted, even if it were real.

Dylan shrugged, then grinned, a look that Serena hadn't seen before.

Nicole led him—not to the bar, but to the fanciest restaurant in the place.

Clearly she wanted the full honeymoon package—the gorgeous ring, the fancy hotel suite, the pricey restaurant. She wanted the memories.

And, poor sap, she'd get them.

Serena waited until the couple followed the maître d' deep into the restaurant. Then Serena checked her appearance, added some lipstick, grabbed her purse, and headed downstairs.

THIRTEEN

Her heart was pounding—not with fear, but with anticipation. She wanted to do this. She wanted it almost as much as she had wanted Dylan that first night.

Serena strode across the hotel, and into the restaurant area. Men who already had a partner tried not to look at her. Men who were alone all smiled as if her appearance gave them hope she would go somewhere with them. Most women gave her the death stare, the one that told her they thought she looked prettier than they did. Other women openly flirted.

She clutched her purse to her side, and entered the restaurant. It smelled of garlic, roasting beef, and freshly baked bread. The maître d' tried to stop her. She gave him her widest smile.

"I'm meeting someone," she said, and pushed past him.

She saw Nicole first. They had a table in the corner. Nicole sat with her back to the wall, her beauty and happiness reflected in the discreet mirrors added just above the chairs to make the room seem bigger.

Dylan sat across from her, his suit coat open, his collar unbuttoned, and his tie loose. He looked like he had already had good sex. Maybe he had, in the car. Or maybe he got satisfied by a con well played.

He sat up as Serena approached, a frown on his face.

Serena made sure she wore a small smile, not a large one. She didn't want to look like the cat that swallowed the canary until all the feathers were in her mouth.

He had just set his napkin down as if he were about to get out of the chair, when she reached him. She slipped her hands inside his suit, down his chest, feeling its familiarity, so flat and perfect. As she did that, she nibbled his ear, then worked her way down his neck, knowing what it did to him.

He gasped just a little, a sexual sound she had forgotten, and tried to move away, but she held him tightly.

"What are you doing?" Nicole demanded. "What's going on?"

Serena kept Dylan in his seat, pressing her breasts against his back, and unbuttoned the front of his shirt near his belt. He reached for her hands, but she slipped them against his warm skin.

She smiled, keeping her mouth against the fragrant side of Dylan's neck. "So this is the new one, Dylan?"

He started at the name.

"Oh, I'm sorry," Serena said, just a little louder. "I meant John. I forget what name he uses on these little excursions."

Nicole's face had gone white. She was looking at Dylan as if she expected him to say something.

The people at the nearby table were watching as well. A waiter, holding a silver ice bucket with a bottle of champagne inside, stood awkwardly by.

"Let me see the ring," Serena said as if she and Nicole were old friends. "He didn't make you buy it, did he? Sometimes he makes the woman buy, and I think that's so rude."

Dylan shoved at her. "Lady, you're crazy."

"I know, my love," she said, sliding her hands down further.

He grabbed her fingers. She could see his face in the mirror. He looked panicked.

Nicole flushed. "Who *are* you?" she snapped at Serena.

"Oh, sweetie," Serena said. "He didn't explain, did he? I'm his wife. We were married years ago. Your marriage isn't legal. The document you signed isn't one that the State of Nevada recognizes, even if the ceremony were performed by a licensed preacher, which yours wasn't. That's just Dylan's—I mean John's—best friend."

"What?" Nicole asked.

"Oh," Serena said, her voice lowering. "Did you marry today? Am I early? You still had a few days of sex left, didn't you? Dylan likes his women to think it's legal. He says it makes them even hotter."

Serena lifted one of her hands and grabbed Dylan's chin tightly. He tried to open his mouth, but she turned his head toward her and kissed him hard.

She pulled her mouth away just enough to say, "My darling loves screwing women. I'm not always able to keep up with him, so I let him roam. Sometimes he gets a bit...involved—"

"I do not!" Dylan finally got some traction. He shoved her backwards. "You damn bitch! What do you think you're doing?"

Her heart was pounding. She hadn't expected him to get so furious.

He raised an arm and was about to hit her, when the waiter dropped the champagne bucket. It sloshed ice everywhere. One of the other diners stood and grabbed Dylan, who struggled against him, screaming obscenities at Serena.

"I'm done with you, you bitch. You have no right to be here! You're *done*."

Her mouth was dry, but she smiled anyway. "Not really. I'm just beginning. I'm going to follow you everywhere, and meet all of your wives. We'll have quite a coven, we wives of the con man named for a poet. We'll—"

"He's a con man?" Nicole was standing, clutching her purse to her chest. "You know he's a con man?"

Everyone looked at her. Water from the ice bucket was sliding across the floor, getting into her shoes, but she didn't even seem to notice.

"He tried to steal everything from me," Serena said.

"You could have *told* me," Nicole said, her voice thick with tears. "You could've stopped the wedding. You could've—"

"It wasn't legal," Serena said. "You're still single—"

Nicole let out a sob and launched herself across the table, pounding Dylan repeatedly with her fists. "You said you *loved* me, you *bastard*. You said—"

"He always says that." A new voice had entered the conversation. Kree stood behind the maître d, wearing an old brown polyester suit coat, and functional pants. She glared at Serena. "Detective Castillo told you to wait."

"And miss this?" Serena smiled. She felt positively giddy.

"It accomplishes nothing." Kree removed a pair of handcuffs from her belt. She expertly snapped the cuffs on Dylan, then dragged him away from the waiter.

"You have no right," Dylan said. "I've done nothing wrong."

Serena gasped at his audacity, but Nicole raised a high heel and kicked. Dylan turned slightly sideways, getting the point of the heel in his thigh.

His eyes narrowed as he said to Nicole, "You were a hell of a lot more fun to screw. I was looking forward to seeing what else you could do."

Nicole screeched and reached for him. Kree moved him even farther away.

Serena knew better than to say anything to Nicole. Serena recognized her pain. Instead, Serena ran a hand along Dylan's face.

"Oh, darling," she said. "You must be slipping. It really didn't take much to convince her that you're the scum of the earth."

His mouth opened in shock, and for a moment, she saw the real man underneath. Panicked, vulnerable, lost. Then his mouth closed and his face flushed. He pursed his lips, and she realized just in time that he was going to spit at her. She barely managed to dodge.

"How very third grade of you," she said. "A real man would apologize."

"For what? Giving you two the best time you've ever had?" he snapped.

Serena tilted her head. "Oh, Dylan, such ego. You always finished a little too fast for me."

He made a growling sound, and Kree yanked him away from her. Another officer had shown up and was helping her.

Nicole had dissolved into a pile of tears. Two of the female patrons had their arms around her as she sobbed.

"I told you to wait." Castillo was standing near one of the tables, arms crossed.

"You sound like Detective Kree," Serena said. She tilted her head at Nicole. "You have a real victim there. You need to deal with her."

"And not the woman who went all vigilante on us?" Castillo's brown eyes missed nothing. She apparently saw the similar dress, the manicure, the haircut.

"I was just going to warn the new wife," Serena lied, "and I got carried away. I'll be happy to come to the station, though, and press charges."

"Tomorrow," Castillo said. "When I'm less pissed at you."

Serena smiled and picked her way out of the mess. Other officers and some security guards were huddled near the doorway. Dylan was being led away. He seemed small now, hunched, as if he'd lost something.

She almost wished she hadn't called the police. She hadn't had that much fun in years. Imagine what it would have been like to follow him from con to con, breaking it up at the exact right moment, having him look over his shoulder, always expecting her to ruin things.

She had planned this a bit too conservatively. She could have done that, and truly ruined him.

She sighed.

The police and the FBI would get enough information from Nicole to arrest the other team members. They'd find the oniony man and the substitute preacher and anyone else who was involved. The entire con would shut down.

The game was over. Serena had won.

She reached for her wedding ring, and started to slip it off. Then she looked at it, the way that Nicole had looked at hers when she got out of the SUV, with wonder and a bit of surprise that it was on her finger.

What was a wedding ring after all, but a trophy? The symbol of a woman who had truly tamed a man.

She closed her left hand into a fist, feeling stronger. Feeling powerful.

Feeling complete for the first time in her entire life.

She hadn't expected this happily ever after when she met Dylan.

But she would take it.

She would take it all.

Afterword

Different Drafts, Different Stories

I love writing short fiction. I start a story and let it unfold beneath my fingers. I never know where it's going to go.

I vividly remember writing what we're now calling the author-preferred edition of "The Wedding Ring." The story came out fast and vicious, rather like the events in the tale.

It's almost a reverse romance. It even has a happily ever after, although not the kind that romances have. Because it has that romance underpinning, the author-preferred version has several sex scenes.

I personally think they enhance the story. They make it clear why Serena fell for Dylan. She also sees the pattern in his behavior with Nicole. The behavior is mostly sexual, because Dylan gets off on his treatment of these women.

He's unnecessarily cruel. But he never sees the result of his cruelty. He leaves while his marks sleep, so he doesn't see the reaction to his abuse of them. In his mind, he can remain the romantic hero he's playing over and over again.

The preferred version is three thousand words longer than the originally published version. Some of those three thousand words are the sex scenes, but much of them are also character development and emotional reaction.

I personally think the published version is a little colder than the preferred version. I think the published version makes Serena a tiny bit less sympathetic.

So why are there two versions?

Because I love the digest mystery magazines. I still enjoy being published by them. The editors there don't buy all of my stories, partly because I push edges. Usually, I just let the chips fall where they may (pun intended), but with this story, I knew what would cause the editors to reject it outright.

There were three factors. The first was the length. Almost no one buys 15,000-word stories for their magazines. That's just too much retail space.

The second reason was the sex scenes. The digests still consider themselves family magazines. So they're a bit stodgy when it comes to sexual content. In fact, I expected the hints of the sex, which had to stay in the story, would probably doom it with the digests anyway.

The third reason was the language. I kept it real in my preferred draft. Some "fucks" and "shits," but also words like "slutty." You can use them all in the digests, but not repeatedly in a story. One editor told me that she got letters whenever there were more than two "fucks" in a short story.

I could trim the swear words (and sometimes do in the versions I send to the digests). If I cut the sex scenes, I made the story short enough to be in the possible range.

So I sent the story out, and heard back from Janet Hutchings at *Ellery Queen's Mystery Magazine*. She loved the story, but it was too long. Could I cut it?

Yowza. I had already trimmed about two thousand words. I

went back in and trimmed more. That was when some of my beloved character details vanished. I trimmed another thousand words, sent it back, and she bought it.

I like the story she published. It's twisty and nasty and true to my vision for the story.

But it lost that romance structure. From the meet-cute to the happily ever after, the romance (or is it anti-romance?) was gone.

That nagged at me. The story came out. It was well received. People liked it. *I* liked it.

But I kept thinking they'd like it more if they read the whole thing.

And now you have. You can figure out for yourself which version you prefer. Writers, you can see what choices I made when I trimmed the story with the editor in mind. You can decide if I did the right thing.

I'm just happy the preferred version is out there. I'm glad I got the opportunity to share it with you.

That's one of the reasons I write, after all. I love to tell myself a story...and then I like to share that story. Not to get other people's reactions, per se, but just to put it out into the world.

I hope you enjoyed this little volume.

I had fun putting it together.

—Kristine Kathryn Rusch
Las Vegas, Nevada
December 12, 2023

Follow Kris on BookBub!

I value honest feedback, and would love to hear your opinion in a review, if you're so inclined, on your favorite book retailer's site.

Be the first to know!

Just sign up for the Kristine Kathryn Rusch newsletter, and keep up with the latest news, releases and so much more—even the occasional giveaway.

So, what are you waiting for? To sign up go to kriswrites.com.

But wait! There's more. Sign up for the WMG Publishing newsletter, too, and get the latest news and releases from all of the WMG authors and lines, including Kristine Grayson, Kris Nelscott, Dean Wesley Smith, *Pulphouse Fiction Magazine,* and so much more.

To sign up go to wmgpublishing.com.

About the Author

An international bestselling editor and writer with over 35 million books in print, Kristine Kathryn Rusch writes in many genres, from mystery to science fiction, from western to romance. She has written under a pile of pen names, but most of her work appears as Kristine Kathryn Rusch. Her Kris Nelscott pen name is highly acclaimed, and her Kristine Grayson pen name became a bestseller in romance. Her science fiction novels set in the bestselling Diving Universe have won dozens of awards and are in development for a major TV show. She also writes the Retrieval Artist sf series and several major series that mostly appear as short fiction.

Her novels have made bestseller lists around the world and her short fiction has appeared in twenty-seven best-of-the-year collections. She has won more than thirty awards for her fiction, including the *Ellery Queen Mystery Magazine* Readers Award, the Hugo, *Le Prix Imaginales*, and the *Asimov's* Readers' Award. Publications from *The Chicago Tribune* to *Booklist* have included her Kris Nelscott mystery novels in their top-ten-best mystery novels of the year. The Nelscott books have received nominations for almost every award in the mystery field, including the best novel Edgar Award, and the Shamus Award.

To keep up with everything she does, go to kriswrites.com and sign up for her newsletter. To track her many pen names and series, see their individual websites (krisnelscott.com, kristinegrayson.com, retrievalartist.com, divingintothewreck.com, pulphousemagazine.com, wmgholidayspectacular.com).

facebook.com/kristinekathrynruschwriter
patreon.com/kristinekathrynrusch
bookbub.com/authors/kristine-kathryn-rusch

www.ingramcontent.com/pod-product-compliance
Lightning Source LLC
Chambersburg PA
CBHW010516100726
47903CB00009B/2778

* 9 7 8 1 5 6 1 4 6 9 5 4 3 *